CHICAGO HUSTLE

ODIE HAWKINS

An Original Holloway House Edition
**HOLLOWAY HOUSE PUBLISHING COMPANY
LOS ANGELES, CALIFORNIA**

Published by
HOLLOWAY HOUSE PUBLISHING COMPANY
8060 Melrose Avenue, Los Angeles, CA 90046

This novel is a work of fiction. Names, characters, places and
incidents are either the product of the author's imagination or are
used fictitiously. Any resemblance to actual events or locales or
persons, living or dead, is entirely coincidental.

International Standard Book Number 0-87067-366-1
Printed in the United States of America
Cover illustration by Glen Tarnowski
Cover design by Bill Skurski

CHAPTER 1

Elijah Brookes stood under the awning in front of the Stickhall, his hat tilted down stylishly over his left eye, his right foot acting as a buttress between himself and the wall behind him, a toothpick casually wobbling from one side of his mouth to the other, as he listened to the man everybody called Monkeydude tell obvious lies to him and two other men.

Monkeydude's latest lie about having been George Raft's bodyguard back in the forties made Elijah smile sarcastically. Who knows what Monkeydude had been? George Raft's bodyguard? Well, he was ugly enough to have been anybody's bodyguard. But, goddamn! Why would he always have to be telling lies that were really so unbelievable? Especially to the cynics who hung out at the Stickhall.

Brotherman, a top-flight cynic, egging Monkeydude on,

asked him, with a sly wink to the others, "Did George Raft let you get off into any of that Hollywood pussy he had locked up, Monk?"

"Did he!? Shiiii-it! Lemme tell you . . . mannnn . . ."

Elijah blotted out Monkeydude's high-pitched voice and the presence of the men around him, as he stared back at the two young white women waiting for the light at the corner to change.

The look that they exchanged was well understood.

Yeahhh, I know what you jive bitches see, Elijah curled his lips down with hip contempt . . . ain't but four of us out here but I bet y'all see a whole bunch o' niggers hangin' 'round outside a poolroom, heehawin' 'n wastin' time.

His curled-down lips altered to form the essence of a smile as the light changed from red to green and back to red again while they stared.

No, it wasn't Monkeydude's story tellin', hoppin' around, diggin' in his ass and laughin' at his own lies that held them. His smile flared slightly.

They were looking at him. He tilted his head back a little, giving the bright afternoon sun a better angle to glance off the smooth planes of his face, and slowly assumed a straddle-legged Shaft-in-the-Ghetto stance so that they could see that he didn't have any shorts on and that he was well hung.

The driver flushed red and suddenly remembered that she was an attractive, young, white brunette driving her girlfriend through the heart of the Southside.

They zoomed off with the next change of the light, trying to re-assume the conventional stiffness they always maintained when driving north on Indiana Avenue, and especially 'round about 47th Street.

Elijah squinted after their car and turned back to the end of Monkey's story.

"Yeahhh, man . . . George Raft was a sho' 'nuff righteous dude."

Elijah shared the indulgent smiles of the men who had graciously granted Monkeydude some b.s. time. What else could you do? There was no way to stop the man from running his mouth, from telling one lie after another.

Brotherman leaned toward Elijah and whispered, con style, "Here come Dee Dee, brotherman."

Elijah winked in reply and threw his toothpick away. A few quick calculations led to one logical decision. What the hell, why not? I won't be meetin' Nick downtown 'til five.

The other men, having spotted Dee Dee Wilson's slow, lush, summer-heavy approach, paused in their actions. Knowing that she was Elijah's thang they didn't want to seem overly interested, but she did have an ass on her that required attention, if it was glanced at from off to the side.

He measured her approach by the surreptitious looks in the eyes of his circle.

Monkeydude, so called because that's what he most closely resembled, took the pregnant pause as an encouragement to begin another embroidery.

"Yeah suhhh, the West Coast, back in the forties, was a pure idee dick head, y'all hear me, a pure idee dick head!"

Elijah took in the full picture of her passing him by, being cool, before he decided to speak.

A hot, sultry Chicago-Southside at 47th and Indiana Avenue type day . . . 38-24-38 . . . Dee Dee Wilson, the best pussy in the neighborhood.

"Where you on your way, Miss Lady?" he slurred at her above the noise of cars honking, record shop music playing and the stream of motherfuckers that spilled from a sucker's mug after being trapped by a shark inside the Stickhall.

Dee Dee turned with an elaborate but graceful movement . . . I'm black and beautiful and I know it.

"Uhhh, oh hi, Elijah."

He felt the impulse to burst into a shrapnel of laughter. Sarcastic. Evil. Cruel. Bullshit. "Uhhh, oh hi, Elijah." Ain't this some shit!?

"I see y'all later on," he signaled to his group and strolled over to Dee Dee, her left hip flexed, their slow movements jelling with the first few steps taken together.

"Damn! I thought you was gon' just shine me on for a minute."

She took a few more steps, negotiating a few familiar cracks in the concrete before answering, wistfully, "You know I wouldn't do that."

"Well, I was just wonderin'," he came back at her smugly, "you act so funny at times."

She gave him her special understanding smile, content to let him spool his little game out.

"How's Leelah?" she asked slyly, after ten more quiet steps together, knowing that she had him for a few hours of this particular afternoon anyway.

"She's awright, I guess," he answered casually. "I haven't seen 'er in a few days."

"That's not what I heard."

Elijah curled his lips down in a familiar expression of disdain. Damn! It sho' would be nice if motherfuckers stayed out of my business. "What did you hear, baby?" he asked, cooling out his urge to leave her with her useless insinuations and go on back to the Stickhall, but . . . what better way could be found to kill off a few hours than with Dee Dee?

"I heard that you all had gone back together, for one thing."

He ignored her comment for a few steps, waved coolly at a sometime hustlin' partner across the street.

"Heyyyy, looka here, Dee Dee, if you dumb enough to believe everything people say . . . well . . ." He shrugged and smiled a deliberately cute li'l smile at her with the corners of his mouth.

Dee Dee melted with the smile and threaded her arm through his. "I don't really pay too much attention to what people be sayin' about you, you know that."

He swept his eyes around in a sneaky review of the streets. Be just my fuckin' luck for Leelah to catch me out here with this bitch hangin' onto my arm.

"I thought you had better sense than to be lettin' people tell you what to think. Remember what I told you . . . believe nothin' that you hear and only half of what you see."

Having tightened it up completely, they continued strolling, both of them knowing that the eventual destination was her apartment.

"Where your kids at?" he asked suavely, yards away from the entrance to her building.

"They over at my mother's place, that's where I was just comin' from," she replied, her eyes down.

Good, he thought, it won't be necessary to make Leonard

and Tischie go out to play.

He nodded, ever so slightly, to the dope fiends sitting on the front stoop. Best thing to do is maintain, no tellin' when one o' these fucked-up motherfuckers might come in handy sometime.

Dee Dee led him up to the third floor, past the topless garbage cans, the blaring soul music, the heavy piss smell and the children playing noisy games in the halls.

"You wanna brew?" she asked him as she unlocked her door.

"Yeahhh, yeah, that sho' would be nice," he mumbled and gracefully slid himself onto the beat-up sofa to the left of the door.

He lapped at Dee Dee's lush behind with his eyes as she walked through the small, cramped apartment to the kitchen. He found it almost impossible to keep a straight face, knowing what was about to go down.

In the summertime they made love sitting on a chair, she draping herself across his lap, or they got it together on the sofa, or went into her small, junky, funky, cluttered bedroom. In the wintertime they always went to the bedroom, especially if she was between boyfriends.

He took his hat off and ruffled his manicured fingers through his semi-curly hair. What the hell was Dee Dee to him? he asked himself as she held the can of beer out to him. A good fuck, he decided easily, watching her settle herself beside him with her own can. But, aside from that, what? A good friend? Yes, that too, if it meant that good friends loaned you money whenever you needed it and you never had to worry about paying them back.

10

"Why you lookin' at me like that?"

"Like what, baby?"

"Like you lookin'."

He pulled a long sip from his can for effect before answering. "I was just thinkin' some pretty things about you, that's all."

"Like what?" she asked with practiced shyness.

"Put your beer down and come closer 'n I'll whisper it in your ear."

She took a big gulp, attempting not to seem too anxious, sat the can down beside the sofa and eased closer.

"What?"

Elijah looked at the curvings of her ear and thought, wowwwww! It's really weird how square some grown-up women try to be. Now here we are, the onliest thing we ever do whenever we get together is fuck . . . and now, here she is, pretending that she wants me to whisper something deep into her goddamned ear.

He gently rimmed the outer ridges of her ear before he allowed the tip of his tongue to slip into the core. Her involuntary shiver told him, once again, that he had touched the money.

He stood up slowly, carefully unbuttoning his shirt.

"Mind if I take off my shirt? It's awfully hot in here."

She surreptitiously checked the doorknob, to make certain that it was in the locked position, and nodded slyly, yes, yes, yes . . . to whatever he wanted to do.

Elijah checked his watch as he bent over to unlace his shoes, shirt and undershirt neatly arranged on a nearby chair. Three o'clock . . . beautiful . . . just enough time.

"What about you, Dee Dee, ain't you hot too, baby?"

She rolled her eyes at him, neither affirming or denying that she was "hot."

He straightened up and suddenly realized that his approach to things had been just a wee bit abrupt. Even if they had been doin' it since high school, on and off, she still expected to be romanced a bit, at times.

He sank down beside her on the sofa, carefully tightening his thirty-year-old stomach.

"I asked you, ain't you hot too, baby?" he whispered as he fondled her breast and kissed her.

"Uhhh huh," she affirmed and stood to take off her skirt and blouse.

Elijah slumped on the sofa and slid his pants off as he watched her striptease.

One thing that was really groovy about Dee Dee, he thought, you never had to bullshit around with her . . . if she wanted to git it on, that's what y'all did. If she didn't, you could run a red-hot poker up her pussy and she wouldn't quiver a false eyelash.

She held her hand out to him with her panties draped around her ankles. "C'mon, let's go in the bedroom," she spoke in a low, clear voice.

Elijah eased into his shoes and tried to make his way out of the bedroom without making any noise.

As usual, he failed. The metal natural comb at the dresser's edge caught his thigh and clattered to the floor.

Dee Dee slowly rolled over onto her back, the sweat-wrinkled sheet draped across her stomach.

"Elijah?"

"Yeah, baby," he answered casually, bending to pick up the comb, hating this part of it all. Damn!

"Why you lie so much?"

He negotiated the few steps around the haphazardly scattered shoes, dirty clothes needing to go to the laundromat or the cleaners, and sat on the side of the bed.

"I ain't lyin', sweetthang . . . I *have* got to meet Nick at five. I told you that, remember? A li'l while ago."

She turned her face to the window, trying to arouse his pity, and mumbled skeptically, "Yeahhh, uhh huh, okay whatever you say."

He stared hatefully at the side of her face for a few seconds, feeling the urge to slam his right fist into it. Why did she, why did women always have to pull this . . . this . . . act?

He softened at the sight of her beautiful brown eyes watering up in the deep afternoon light. He leaned over and shoveled her shoulders up into his arms.

"Dee Dee, don't be this way, baby . . . you know I wouldn't leave if I didn't have to. You know that, don't you?"

He frowned over her shoulder as her arms gripped him around the neck and smeared tears on his shirt front.

"I know you have to go, it's just that . . . it's just that I don't really get a chance to see you 'cept every now 'n then."

He held her back from his shirt front, feeling compassion in spite of himself. "I know, baby . . . I know. But you know how it is, thangs'll be movin' so fast sometimes that I don't really have too much of a chance, sometimes . . . to

13

be doin' what I really would like to be doin'.''

Dee Dee nodded agreeably, knowing that it was all bull-shit, designed to ease his exit and give her something to hang onto for next time. He kissed her and pulled himself out of her embrace a few throbs away from getting back into bed with her.

"I gotta get on my job, baby . . ." he whispered with a definite move and stood up.

She blew a kiss at him and cocked her right leg lascivi-ously as he turned to take one last look at her from the bedroom door.

"See you later on," he signed to her and retrieved his hat from the sofa on his way out.

Closing the door softly, he almost sighhhed . . . beauti-ful, I got away clean.

He checked his watch . . . 4:18 p.m. . . . groovy . . . just enough time.

He froze off the attention given him by his friends as he walked quickly past the Stickhall.

"Awww, you don't know us now, huh? . . . now that you done gone 'n got yo' nuts off."

He felt no need to reply to Brotherman's comment, what was ahead was more important and he was already wheeling his attention around to it.

On the El heading downtown, his consciousness flick-ered, as it often did when he was going to run a game, from the game to what he had just finished doing.

He smiled at his reflection in the El window. What could be better preparation for anything than fuckin'?

He held his hand out in front of him slightly, studied it

14

and smiled again. Pussy calms you down.

Dee Dee Wilson. We could've really been into something if she hadn't got herself all fucked up. First, one accident, then another accident and finally, some fool says "Ahhh luvvv you, baybeee," and you off to the races again, minus his love and support because after he had gotten his "luvvv" thang satisfied, he was off to new fields. Yeahhh, Dee Dee, I can understand you trying to hang around my neck, if I had had as many bitches break my heart, as you've had dudes, I think I'd try to hang on too.

Elijah snorted and sucked phlegm down his throat. Damn . . . wish I had some more coke . . . that was some nice girl Monkeydude had. Maybe Nick'll have some.

He popped up at his stop, pleased to see the early birds, the fifteen minute to five guys, rushing onto the El, anxious to get back to their necks of the woods.

Yeahhh, the more the merrier.

He took the steps to the streets two at a time, feeling full, masculine, hip, happy, in a way, to be on his job.

He strolled the block to the first place he and Nick the Geech planned to do, studying the shapely bodies passing him by, the square clothes draped on the flabby shapes of the white businessmen.

Nick stood off to one side of the entrance to the department store, checking his watch four times as Elijah walked up. "Dahm!" he muttered in his sometimes thicker 'n than other times Jamaican accent, "it's aboat time," as they pushed their way through a traffic hour, five o'clock horde of consumers. They separated after entering, two brown-skinned, medium tall, slender, well-dressed black men.

They moved in a counterclockwise fashion, casually taking note of the most crowded sales places, where the clerk salesperson was catching hell.

With a simple glance, to indicate where the action was going to come off, Elijah eased into the small group herded around a harassed salesgirl at the lingerie counter.

He picked up two pairs of sheer black panties and a pair of panty hose, edged up into the small crowd around the salesgirl and, insistently but pleasantly, held his purchases out to be charged for.

Nick, meanwhile, taking note of Elijah's buy, picked the same set of items and circled to the opposite side of the counter, pushing himself belligerently in front of several ladies who were doing some pushing themselves. He timed his impatience to the moment the salesgirl touched Elijah's purchases.

"Goddamn, Miss! Am I gon' t' ever get waited on?! I been tryin' t' get your attention for the last ten minutes! What're you tryin' to do? Ignore me or something?"

The women around Nick bristled up. They were middle-aged white ladies and afraid of black men, period . . . and didn't want to create a scene.

The salesgirl, younger and more positive about her attitudes, chewed on one corner of Nick's ass with a brief, cold look and gave him some advice.

"Hold your water, Mister, I only have two hands and no pots."

Elijah thanked her as she gave him his change from a ten-dollar bill, smiling at her sympathetically and at the put-down Nick had just received.

"Now sir, what can I do for you?" Elijah heard the sales-girl say as he drifted away.

"He wasn't furst, I wuz," a little, wizened black lady spoke up and handed her items over to the salesgirl.

Elijah circled the first floor of the store, waiting for Nick to get waited on, checked out the prices on a number of items he planned to cop in the near future.

Finally, noting that Nick had been waited on, he headed for the men's room. Nick walked in seconds later, mumbling obscenities. "Mahnnn, ah'm tellin' ya, these bitches really irri-tate me left nut at times!"

They exchanged packages, each of them stapled with the sales ticket at the top, a clever way to prevent thieves from putting more into the bag than they had paid for.

Elijah squeaked, Flip Wilson-Geraldine style, "He wasn't furst, I wuz," as he made his exit.

Nick the Geech smiled at his partner's humor and leaned close to the mirror. Dahm blackheads! Gotta start gettin' facials more often.

Elijah strode through the store with a straight look about him, as though he were on his way to right a wrong.

He waited patiently through three customers at the lingerie counter.

"Yessir?" the salesgirl smiled brightly at him, liking the hat, his pea-green see-through shirt, despite the smudge on the front, the whole, hip, black fashion effect of him. "May I help you? Back for more goodies?"

Elijah pushed back his urge to smile at where she was coming from . . . like, this was sho' 'nuff business and no time to be jivin'.

"I hope you can help me, Miss . . . I gave you a twenty-dollar bill a few minutes ago, for these items." He held the bag up as though he were doing a minor league medicine show bit.

Nick smiled at the performance from the far side of the store.

The salesgirl frowned, remembering him and his ten-dollar bill. It had been a ten-dollar bill, she was certain of it. "May I see your sales receipt, sir?" she asked coldly.

Elijah took a deep breath . . . time for the moment of lie. "My sales receipt!" he nutted up on her, loudly. "My sales receipt! For what!? I'm tellin' you I gave you a twenty and you only gave me change for a ten and you wanna try to put me through a lotta changes. What kinda place is this?!"

Nick frowned, looking around in the pocketbook section. It was always a drag when attention had to be called to the performance, lots of times the salesgirl would just simply give it up after a little hesitation . . . this was one of those assholes trying to protect the company's money. Nick frowned again at the salesgirl. Bitch should be caned. And smiled at Elijah waving his arms around like a nut.

Several people, nice, clean-cut, home-made types, stopped to watch the angry black man.

"I shouldn't have to show my receipt . . . I'm an honest man, I work for my money! I'm tellin' you, I didn't get my right change. You didn't . . ."

The salesgirl, suspecting some kind of game, but not hip to what it might be, cut him off.

"Sir, I'll have to call the floor manager."

"Hey! I don't care who you call! All I want is the rest of my change! I work too hard for my money to be giving it away."

The salesgirl ignored him and signaled to a small penguin-shaped figure of a man with a flower in his buttonhole, strolling by with his hands clasped behind his back.

"Mr. Morrison . . . uh, Mr. Morrison! Counter four, please."

Elijah stood slightly off to one side, his nostrils flared out. Morrison looked at Elijah with the look he reserved for Chicanos, Blacks, Indians and other obviously inferior people.

"Yes, what is it, Mizz Jenkins?"

Elijah caught Nick's worried expression from the corner of his eyes, and signaled to him with a positive gesture that everything was going good.

"Mr. Morrison, this gentleman purchased some items a short time ago . . ."

Elijah held his package up as Exhibit A.

"And he says I gave him the wrong change."

Morrison, an old hand at making adjustments, took out a small white pad. "Yes?" he lisped.

"Well . . . well, I'm almost certain I gave him the right change. He gave me a ten-dollar bill, his items were $4.85, and I gave him the right change!" she closed off aggressively.

"Look, Miss . . . I told you. Now if I've told you once, I've told you a dozen times, you didn't . . ."

Morrison, a smug expression on his narrow face, held up both shapely hands pontifically.

"May I see your sales receipt, sir?"

Elijah glared at the salesgirl and pretended that he was about to search his pockets.

Morrison, patronizing the childlike mentality of the forgetful black, reached over delicately and took the store's brown bag, with the sales receipt stapled to the top, out of Elijah's hand. "May I?"

Morrison quickly noted that the sales receipt showed that the change for a twenty should have been given.

"I'm afraid you have made a misthake, Mizz Jenkins." He passed the bag over for her to look at, vaguely pissed because of the hassle it had caused.

"I . . . I'm sorry, Mr. Morrison, I could've sworn . . ."

Elijah, the gallant winner, winked and rapped.

"Ain't no big thang. I just knew I had paid you with a twenty because . . . hahhhahhahh . . . it was the only one I had. My woman almost ripped it out of my hand yesterday, wantin' it for something else, so I had to whip a li'l piece a tape across the split."

The salesgirl pursed her lips skeptically, anxious to go and take care of other customers. So maybe he was right, but she still didn't believe it.

Morrison, feeling the need to assert his power, chewed on Mizz Jenkins a li'l bit.

"We're not paying you to establish store policy, Mizz Jenkins. Your job is to give our customers the best possible service. Please refund this gentleman hith proper change and make the necethary corrections on your regithter. Sorry for the inconvenience, sir."

"Aww, like I said before," Elijah announced grandly, "ain't no big thang."

20

Nick took a deep breath as he watched the floor manager go one way, and Elijah the opposite way, after the salesgirl had counted his change out.

Nick started for the exit. Shit gets on my left nerve sometimes, or maybe I'm gettin' old.

Miss Jenkins followed Elijah's jaunty exit as she turned her attention to a waiting row of customers.

She rang the first sale up and quickly leafed through the twenty-dollar bills in her cash register drawer as she made change. The frown distorted her features painfully.

"Anything wrong, my dear?" the little old lady she was making change for asked.

"Oh, nothing, nothing," she answered, carefully counting change out into the little old lady's hand, puzzled, puzzled, puzzled.

Elijah and Nick walked quickly to the next downtown corner, the next huge department store complex.

"Why did it take so long to get over?" Nick asked from the corner of his mouth, con style.

"I'll tell you about it later, I don't want to break my concentration now."

Nick rolled his eyes around, expressing absolute skepticism, but who could complain? Elijah was a winner, always on his job, and you never had to worry about not gettin' into something, maybe his concentration helped.

After all, he was the one who had figured out how much you could make, just playing five stores for a li'l taste from each one of them. Say you started off with a base thirty bucks, ten to one and twenty to the other. Running the short change game, even for chump change, was likely to fill your pockets up . . .

Elijah had made a believer out of Nick the Geech by running the chump change-into-grand-theft-dough game down to him. "See, dig it Nick, lotsa dudes make the big moves, get busted and that's all she wrote. My way is steady and pretty goddamned well organized, if I do say so myself.

"Here's how it works: with the twenty-dollar switch, with the change comin' from it, we can wind up with between forty-five 'n seventy-five bucks for an hour's work, between the hours of five 'n six, you know, right in the middle of the rush hour . . . and during Christmas time 'n holidays like that . . . shit! we clean up. Think about it. One hour's work a week, if you only score for the minimum, that's what? Two hundred twenty-five bucks. If you come away with the maximum, that's three hundred seventy-five . . . now then, if you only manage to come off with the minimum for six months, half a year . . . well, you can see."

Nick had seen, was seeing and working at it. It was his turn to return to the salesgirl for the change she had forgotten to give him.

She was nice as pie.

"Oh, sorry, I guess it just isn't my day."

Nick smiled indulgently, stuffed the change into his pocket, and casually strolled past Elijah, on their way to the next one. They practically yawned their way through the last number, feeling cocky, at ease, with the practice of a string of four stings behind them.

"Dig, brother Geech, you gon' have to get your indignation thang together a li'l bit better."

Elijah started into his critique as they filed through the cafeteria line of Bowman's in the basement, a favorite of the fast and semi-fast people on the loop track.

"How so?" Nick asked, studious lines across his forehead, beating Elijah to a choice piece of apple pie.

"Well, the way you came up on the broad the third time, for example. The bitch was supposed to be feelin' so threatened by your nigger nasty-ass behavior that she damn near forgets she countin' change out to me . . . but that ain't what happened 'cause you had let your energy level drop too low."

"Uhh huh, I dig whot you're sayin', I got t' be the nigger they think I am, the unloved one, and you be the loved one."

Elijah stabbed the back of Nick's head with both eyes as they went through the checkout station, barely able to contain himself.

"Look, man!" he talked urgently across the cafeteria table into Nick's face, "I don't give a fuck how them people feel about me. All I know is this, in order to play on how they minds work, we got to have our shit up tight. Can you dig where I'm comin' from, brotherman?"

Nick spooned up a heap of bland macaroni. "Hey mahn, you know I'm just jivin'. The name of the game is success."

He reached his free hand over for Elijah to slap, and started into the assorted plates on his tray in earnest, wishing that there was some goat meat on one of them.

Elijah studied his movements for a few seconds. That's the groovy thang about Nick the Geech, he takes every fuckin' thing seriously. They nodded to the regulars smoking their after-dinner cigarettes, on their way out, bellies puffed out, wallets fat.

"Well, that's what that was. They don't have good food but at least it fools you into being full."

Nick slapped his palm and looked over his shoulder at the cafeteria entrance, disdainfully.

"Yeahhh, you can say that again."

A moment of mutual good feeling passed between them, taking in the balmy Chicago air.

"Think I'm gon' call it a day, bruh Nick . . . I feel almost like I been workin'."

"Yeah, I'll bet," Nick slid in slyly, signifyin'. "Somebody tol' me they saw Dee Dee rip you off the corner. I had doubts about us gittin' down when I heard . . ."

"Ain't been a piece o' pussy slit that would keep me from takin' care business. And Lawd knows Dee Dee has sho' 'nuff got a good 'un."

"How long you and that broad been into it?"

Elijah followed the woman's body passing by with an expert's interest. Forty-two, three, on her last legs but still tryin' to look good. Too bad she didn't do some sit-ups when she was younger, it might've kept her belly from hangin' down between her legs like that.

"What did you say, man?"

"Yeah, that bitch sho' has got a helluva turdcutter on it, ain't she?" Nick contributed his own esthetic considerations. "I was askin' how long you 'n Dee Dee had been into it?"

Elijah smiled slightly. Nick would love to fuck Dee Dee,

I know he would.

"Awww man, ever since I was in high school. I dropped out in my second year, she graduated, shacked up or married a couple times, nobody really knows, had a couple crumbcrushers and we ain't never stopped doin' it durin' all that time. I just don't seem to be able to cut the bitch loose."

Nick adjusted his hat, preparing to get on off into Saturday. "Well, if you ever decide to, let me have first shot."

Elijah gave his hustlin' partner a quick, understanding wink. Like, hey nigger, you ain't gon' never get none o' the pussy if you expect me to ever step aside 'n let you in.

"Uhh huh, riight on!" he mumbled. "You goin' back down on the block?"

"Yeahhh, I was thinkin' 'bout playin' a li'l poker tonight. What're you up to?"

Elijah started backing away, wanting to move, his blood still alive from the day's games.

"I don't know, a li'l this 'n a li'l that."

"Right on!" Nick winked, made a clenched fist, Black Power salute in a tight arch at the chest level, and started for the nearest El station.

Elijah watched him, dipping a bit in the knees, body alert for whatever, mind even sharper, heading for the Southside, and some barbeque, probably.

Elijah accidentally released a sound as he smiled about the way his friend functioned in the world. Good ol' Nick the Geech . . . couldn't find too many like him. You could pull it off with him 'cause he knew how to play. Yeahhh, he was a player.

A stern-faced, white-haired white man in a mackinaw shirt and a straw hat smiled indulgently at Elijah in his, to his mind, funny clothes, as they passed each other on the steps of the train station, one coming, the other going.

Elijah methodically checked the usual nesting spots of the station's detectives. His eyes went from track No. 16 to No. 20 on the left and from No. 1 to No. 9 on the right . . . he spotted the one he and Brotherman had nicknamed Dolores because he was such a punk that he didn't even know it himself.

He brushed Dolores away with a thought. He'll probably be goin' off into the men's toilet in a couple minutes to see if he can catch a couple of these gay commuters playin' with each other's li'l pink peckers. And besides, he's on the other side of the shopping plaza.

He took one last sweep before reaching the ground level. Beautiful, nobody treacherous in sight.

Keeping an I-got-a-purpose-here look on his face, he dug through his pockets in the wall locker storage section, opened one of the lockers and pulled out his "grab bag." The house bricks inside the valise gave his arm just the right amount of strain when he picked it up.

The grab bag. He had to do it fast because they all knew him at the station. Sometimes, when he was high, and consequently invisible, he knew that they couldn't see him, but he wasn't high now, although he really wanted to be.

As usual, it popped up in front of him as though someone had deliberately placed it there.

With that sly, all-encompassing look that allowed him to see everybody in a room full of people all at once, he swept the station floor, checking out every face that might seem to be checking him, even as he watched the tall, erect, well-dressed white dude head for the schedule-of-departure board. Satisfied that it was cool, he stood near the suitcase the man had left sitting in the middle of the station.

Elijah sometimes felt like the only man in the world when he did the grab bag ... because it was as though everyone knew what he was doing, and out of the hundreds milling around, it seemed only natural that someone would scream on him, but so far, in three years straight, he had only been paranoided out of his game five times.

He took a deep breath as he bent slightly and placed his suitcase near the expensive number. Beautiful, just about the same size.

It didn't matter if the color were different, that was cool ... from a distance the mark would think he had misplaced his bag and be bewildered just long enough for Elijah to cut a corner and be gone.

He paused in the magazine section, set the suitcase down and browsed through *Players* for a full fifteen minutes, his heart skipping against his chest like a wet towel.

His whole self wanted to be trotting up the stairs to the outside, to a cab, but he knew from experience that that's how dudes got caught a lot of times ... they'd start rushing up the steps like they were going to catch a train, and what they never remembered ... the white man wasn't stupid, any nigger running up any stairs, anywhere, had to be up to no good.

Finally, calmed down and feeling supercool, he started up the stairs, being careful to pause after every few steps, to allow his hands and wrists a rest from their heavy burden.

Outside the station he hailed a cab and felt such a sense of power that he felt tempted to go back and exchange the valise he had for somebody else's.

"Where you wanna go, man?" the cab driver, a working man, looked up in the mirror at the man of wits and sneered.

"Forty-seventh 'n King Drive, good brother," Elijah answered him quietly. Didn't do too much good to get egotistical with cab drivers, they could help you out sometimes, in different ways.

He looked at the grab bag closely. Nice grained leather, expensive make. Wowwww! I really got one today.

He watched the shading of the people, of the neighborhoods change . . . from the brick, metal and glass world of where he had gone to feed, so to speak . . . turn to the rich, soft, lush velvet of black people getting ready to do a beautiful summer Saturday night number. At 43rd Street, he started thinking about what he was going to wear and where he was going to style it off. Maybe with Leelah. I know she's probably home by now.

CHAPTER 2

He eased into the room behind the sound of Coltrane, checked out the trio of clock radios, the chair with six expensively tailored suits flopped across the back, the two portable television sets, both color, and the wooden box with the wristwatches in it on the dresser. All thieved for.

Leelah Dobbs was sprawled out flat on her belly, talking on the telephone as usual, he noted.

He closed the door softly, sat the grab bag down and looked closely at his main lady. Small, brown, fine. An old slash mark running from her left ear to her cheekbone made a spectacular dimple when she smiled . . . a thug bitch if ever there was one, both of them out of the same can of worms.

"Hey, look! fool!" she growled into the receiver after having obviously listened to enough bullshit, "don't be givin' me all that static! You can talk to him about it . . . he just walked in."

"Who is it?"

"That simple assed Leo," she spoke past the receiver, wanting Leo to know what she thought of him.

"Hey Leo, what's happenin'?"

"Saaayyy, looka here, bruh . . . I heard what yo' woman said 'bout me!" Leo slurred into Elijah's ear.

"Skip all that, what's happenin'?"

"Awwww, uhhh . . . awright, dig it. I done dropped three o' those bullets I . . . uhhh . . . copped from you yes-ta-day and I don't feel. Git no kinda feelin' at all. I don't feel shhhiiit!"

"You a motherfuckin' lie, Leo! If you didn't feel nothin' you wouldn't be callin' me to tell me about it."

"You . . . uhhh . . . you . . . thank I'm trippin', huhhh?"

"You goddamned right you trippin'! Now git outta my ear with this bullshit!"

"Yeeeahhhh, uhhh huh, awright, Mr. Elijah, you the boss."

"Take care, Leo . . . I'll catch you later on." He hung up and spoke casually to Leelah, like a man coming home from his job. "Hey sweetthang, what's to it?"

Leelah lit a cigarette and let her bottom lip out slightly more than necessary exhaling.

"I thought you said you was gon' call me this afternoon?"

Elijah rolled his eyes up to the ceiling, faking disgust.

"Now come on, Leelah! Don't be givin' me a hard time! I got three shifts o' police ticklin' me in the ass, a whole boatload o' crazy motherfuckers tryin' to git into my head and a whole bunch of other thangs weighin' me down. The *last* thing I need is some square bitch bullshit about 'you was 'sposed to call at noontime!' "

Leelah withdrew her bottom lip slightly, her bluff called. "Well, you said you was! I didn't ask you to."

Elijah, realizing that the challenge had been met, relaxed his stance. "Yeah! yeahhh, well, I couldn't. I was tied up," and checked the goods cluttering up the apartment.

Leelah made a remark, half to herself, half to him, "You always tied up" . . . that he ignored.

"What is all this shit still doin' here? I thought you 'n Zelma was 'sposed to be gettin' rid o' this shit?"

Leelah rolled over onto her back, bullshit past, taking care of business now.

"I got in touch with Browney and he said he wouldn't be able to handle it 'til Monday. Unless . . . hahhahhah . . . you wanted to do a credit thing with him."

"Credit?! Credit what?!"

Leelah smirked, knowing her man.

"You know, he would have the stuff picked up and pay you Monday. I told 'im you wouldn't go for it."

"You told 'im right, baby! You know somethin'? I think that honky been dealin' with in-sane niggers so long that he thinks we all crazy. Well, we definitely gon' have to clean house pretty soon, fo' real. You checked it out? Li'l Bit 'n him is hangin' 'round like buzzards."

"Uh huh, really! Like I said, he told me he'd be able to take care business Monday, for sure. Whatchu got in the grab bag?"

Elijah hefted the suitcase onto the bed beside her. "Let's

see ." He broke the flimsy lock with a shoe heel and opened the suitcase slowly, silently hoping that it would be filled with money.

"Wowww! Looks like you hit the jackpot today, brother."

The two of them looked over the contents of the suitcase with seasoned, trader's eyes.

A couple well-tailored suits, two expensive German cameras, and the usual assortment of traveler's clothes.

"Dude must be into photography."

Leelah pulled both of the cameras out and weighed one in each hand. "I know a dude who'll take both of these 'n give a good price."

Elijah stood up to try on one of the suitcoats. "Cool, take 'em."

"Thought you said you were goin' after women's things for a while?"

"Gotta take what the good Lord sends, baby. Don't worry, you gon' always get yours. Nice fit, huh?"

"I've seen better," she replied, a little of her petulence returning.

Elijah draped the coat across the end of the bed and sat down beside her for a kiss. She turned her head away slightly.

"I saw Dee Dee this evenin' and she spoke to me for the first time in a month, even had the nerve to try to smile, with her bucktooth self!"

Elijah permitted himself a dry smile. Women!

"You say that to say what?"

"I ain't sayin' that to say nothin'. I just don't want that bitch laughin' 'n grinnin' in my face."

He made a spontaneous decision to defuse the situation. "Awww goddamn! Leelah! pull your ass off your shoulder! You talk like she's my woman or somethin'!"

"Y'all fuckin' every chance you git, ainchu?"

Elijah turned his face toward the window, as though he had suddenly seen something. It never paid to be too flip with Leelah. If the shit started smelling, Leelah Dobbs would be the first one to say it stank, and wouldn't stutter over one single word.

Having failed with the defusing, he decided to nutroll. "Baby, we got any more o' that good smoke left?"

Leelah felt tempted to laugh in his face. How many times had he shot her off to another place when she was pressing him? How many different ways?

"Yeahhh, we still got some," she sighed, on the verge of giving up. She moved to the closet with her usual quick, precise movements, pulled a shoebox out and handed it to Elijah.

"'Lijah, you still didn't answer my question."

"What question was that, baby?" he asked, smiling up at her innocently.

"You and Dee Dee got a thang goin' on, ainchu?"

Elijah expertly, efficiently rolled one, lit it, toked up and passed it to her as he took off his shirt. Leelah noticed the slight smudge over the left pocket. Mascara.

"We ain't got no bigger thang goin' on than you 'n Zelma," he replied finally, sprawling back on the bed, the first effects of the dynamite seeping in.

They stared at each other evenly for a few seconds, faces carefully arranged to say nothing or everything, and then, spontaneously, they lapsed into mutual grins and fell into each other's arms.

"Elijah Brookes! What am I gon' do with you?!"

He began to struggle out of his pants. "I already got one thing in mind."

She stood up and began to disrobe.

Elijah smiled and thought to himself . . . doubleheaders can wear you out. Oh well . . . my dick'll rot away one day, may as well use it as much as I can now.

Leelah and Elijah sat at one of their favorite tables in the Tiger Lounge, drinking Afro-gins, waiting for the house group to come back on, feeling good from love and a long, sexual catnap, enjoying their kind of people . . . stuff players, second story men, petty drifters, fast steppers, dope fiends, ho's 'n pimps.

Leelah nudged Elijah, alerted him to the fierce little dialogue going on between Dot the ho and her man, Precious Percy.

"Now, Dot . . . I done clocked you! You been sittin' on your ass for the last eighteen minutes, tappin' your foot and drinkin'."

"I'm waitin' for somebody, Precious," she replied meekly.

"You go wait for 'somebody' outside. Now what I'm gon' do is this . . . I'm goin' to the toilet, to let some water out of this fine hose of mine, and when I come out . . . I don't wanna see yo' lazy, triflin' ass nowhere in sight. Dig it?"

Dot practically bowed from the waist on the bar stool, losing her balance. "Awright, Precious . . . awright, baby."

Precious Percy frowned stiffly at Dot to re-emphasize his point and turned to stroll to the men's room, to refreeze his nose.

"What it is, Precious? What it is?" Elijah spoke out to him as he passed their table.

Precious shrugged and shook his head negatively, showing with every gesture how rough times were.

"You got it, bruh 'Lijah, you got it, man."

Elijah watched Percy disappear into the men's room at the back of the club. Precious Percy, the pimp, the ladies' good time grinder and weak spot finder. His mind flashed across the pimp's life and decided against it again. And besides, if it wasn't for the fact that pimpin' sisters was becoming more and more unpopular, being thirty years old was a helluva late time to start.

The house group returned to the set. Junkie bassist, an ex- with almost everybody from Horace Silver to Stevie Wonder. Drums kicked by an undiscovered Art Blakely, rumored to be a speed freak, and from the way he played, sometimes, it was believable. Piano player hung up on a lost chord, a trumpet player who could've played higher but was dedicated to getting down to those burnt, deep moods that the middle Miles Davis owned. They swirled into action . . . "ah one ah two, ah one two three . . ."

They settled back. Leelah draped her arm around the back of Elijah's chair. Her man. She looked at his profile as he nodded in time to the music.

Elijah Brookes was going to be in the big time someday, she knew it in her bones, if she had anything to do with it. How much did they have saved? Thirty-five hundred bucks . . . a few more grand and they could get into some kind of legitimate business, maybe buy a car, do something.

Elijah felt her looking at him, smiled out of the corner of his mouth and squeezed her thigh under the table. Uhh huh . . .

They both laughed at the sight of the bass player being jabbed out of a longer than usual nod by the drummer. The drummer had done it so quick that a lot of the people missed it.

Cleotis Murphy and Homer Jackson slid in as they listened to the bassman run through a deep, involved, bass solo, the mysteries of a junkie's musical dream.

Cleotis Murphy and Homer Jackson. The message was sent and received with one quiet rush . . . two of the baddest black motherfuckers around, who also happened to be detectives.

The wheelers and dealers in the Tiger didn't stop wheeling and dealing, they just took their swift moving actions to a slower, more cautious place.

Elijah slipped Leelah his piece, a little Italian job that he carried when they went out, just to keep the wolves at bay.

Murphy and Jackson, strolling the length of the log, caught the surreptitious actions being performed because of their appearance. "What you doin', brother Brookes, cleanin' up?"

Elijah smiled easily. "Cleanin' up? Cleanin' up what, Officer Murphy?"

The two detectives exchanged broad smiles with each other, knowing that damned near everybody in the club was dirty in some way, and took seats at the bar for a couple of on duty drinks.

The members, like some kind of game that realizes that the lion in its midst has killed, eaten and is no longer a threat, returned to their various businesses.

At the conclusion of the group's third number, being given a big round of applause for "Filthy McNasty," Elijah spotted a face peeking through the window beyond the neon, signalling to him.

He looked toward the women's toilet, half a mind on Leelah in the toilet and what she would think when she found him gone and half on what the face signaling to him wanted.

Instinct gave him the answer to his problem ... he moved.

"Leavin' so soon, Mr. Brookes," Murphy signified with him.

"Yeah, you goin'? Don't do anything I wouldn't do," his partner added.

Elijah smiled indulgently at both of them and kept on steppin'.

"Psssst! pssssst! 'Lijah! over here, man!"

Elijah made a disdainful face. Benny the Bone, Bony Benny, sometimes known as Benny the Bandit. What the hell did he want?

He eased up to Benny in the shadows of a hallway four doors from the lounge.

"Heyyyy, what's happenin', 'Lijah? I called your crib and didn't get no answer, so I figured you'd be down here. I didn't wanna come inside 'cause Murphy 'n Jackson been harassin' me all week."

"Yeah, I can dig it. Them two crazy motherfuckers just

made the scene a few minutes ago. I was gettin' ready to git on myself. What's happenin'?"

Benny, anxious to prolong the suspense, to tighten his game, lit a cigarette and exhaled slowly.

"I got a lead pipe cinch . . . you game?"

Elijah's voice dripped with skepticism as he asked coolly, "Game? Ooohh, I don't know, run it down to me."

"Okay, dig this!" Benny talked urgently from the shadows. "I just got word from a buddy who was there, about one o' those heavyweight crap games goin' on, over on the Westside."

"What you plannin' to do, palm some dice and get your throat cut?"

Benny, not one to be insulted by anyone, responded, "Naw, nawww, not really. But I was just thinkin'. There must be other ways to . . . uh ruh . . . get some of that bread, if not all of it. All I need is somebody with some heart to back me up . . . so, quite naturally, I thought about you."

Elijah studied Benny's expression for some sign of bullshit, found none, but continued his skeptical probing. "Uhhn huh. All we have to do is just bust in and get our asses kicked."

"Not likely, blood . . . with them on they bellies, with they asses heisted up in the air. Just think man! For five grand or more! My man told me he had blown three bills himself before he cut out."

"Five grand, huh?"

Benny nodded affirmatively, emphatically.

Elijah pursed his lips, carefully reviewing the dangers

connected to robbing a crap game. It was a little bit like winner take all. The loser would have nothing, and there was nothing that they could legally do about it.

The big problem was the big "If" involved with trying to jam fifteen or twenty dudes who did a lot of jamming themselves.

"What kinda heat you got?"

Benny's eyes glittered a little in the shadows as he recited the pieces in his armory. "Sawed-off shotgun, two .45s and a luger."

"How much did you say was in the game?"

"How much? At least five grand. Probably more by now."

Elijah spun the whole business around in his skull once more, whipping through the ifs and ands, the buts and wherefors. "I'll take the shotgun," he announced coldly.

"Yeahhh, cool! that's cool with me!" Benny moved completely out of the shadows, grinning with his rat-pointed teeth.

"We split the take right down the middle, right?"

"Right on! blood! right on!"

"And if I get robbed tomorrow," Elijah added, knowing Benny's ways, "by anybody . . . anybody. I'm comin' for your ass."

Benny tried to look shocked, but failed. He shrugged nonchalantly instead. "Right on!"

His mind made up, Elijah prepared to move. "Wait here a minute, lemme go back 'n tell Leelah I'm makin' a run."

He took a few steps in the direction of the club and suddenly reversed his field, Murphy and Jackson on his mind.

"Fuck it! She'll know I'm gone when she misses me.

Let's git on!"

"Come on, I'm parked 'round the corner here."

They loped off to Benny's ride, Elijah pumping him for as much information as possible.

Leelah sat at their table, her jaws becoming tighter with each passing minute. Finally, completely bugged, she approached one of the regulars.

"Danny baby, would you go into the men's toilet and see if Elijah is constipated or somethin'?"

Danny looked past Leelah's head sheepishly, wishing she had asked someone else, knowing her bad temper. "Uhh, he ain't in the . . . uhh . . ."

"Well, where in the fuck is he then?" she asked loudly.

"He split, baby," Detective Murphy answered, half turning on his stool.

She gritted her teeth and signalled to the waitress for another drink, muttering savagely to herself the whole while. "Dirty rotten black ass motherfucker . . . can't even go out for a minute without showing his ass!"

Benny drove extra carefully, feeling proud to have a bonafide player on his j.o.b. with him.

"Heyyy man, I got some dynamite smoke with me, can you handle it?"

Elijah stared at Benny's profile for a long moment, almost hating him. Could he handle it? shit!

"I'm a thoroughbred, motherfucker. What do you mean, can I handle it?"

Benny glanced at Elijah's hard expression to make certain he hadn't stirred up any bad, bad vibes and smiled a conciliatory smile.

"I hear ya, I hear ya, bruh."

He pulled two finger-sized joints out of his breast pocket, handed Elijah one.

"It'll be a cinch, man. All we have to do is put some cover over our faces, walk in, push these fools down on the floor, rip 'em off 'n git in the wind."

Elijah sucked home a couple times before responding to Benny's oversimplified con.

"Sounds like a winner to me. I just hope we don't have happen to us what happened to Juneboy last year." ·

Benny released a high-pitched giggle, loaded already. "What happened?"

Elijah smiled out at the lights of the city sweeping past him, the warm summer air brushing his face. High again.

"Uhh, what happened, man?"

Elijah pulled back from his personal thoughts and went to entertainment for Benny's sake, knowing that he needed some kind of fun session to cool him out, build up his shaky morale.

"June broke in on some cold-blooded dudes with no bullets in his piece. One of the dudes called his bluff, took his piece, what little money he had, stuffed boot in his ass and pushed him back out on the streets with nothin' but his socks 'n shorts on . . . and it was two degrees colder than a well digger's asshole."

Benny's nervousness made his high-pitched sniffling sound almost hysterical. "Yeahhh, that sho' was cold!"

Elijah allowed himself a self-indulgent chuckle before settling back to the business at hand. A gambling house robbery could be a super tricky proposition if it wasn't handled right.

"Uhh, lemme check the piece that I'm gon' use out."

"Look in the back seat, wrapped up in that towel. Box o' shells in the glove compartment."

Elijah broke the piece down and checked it out carefully, hesitated to load it for a second, but then decided to. No telling what kind of response a bunch of gambling house tough nuts would make, best be ready.

Benny wrestled the car into a parking space.

"You all right, man?" Elijah asked him.

Benny nodded. "How 'bout yourself?"

"I'm cool. That really is some bad smoke though."

"I told you."

They sat in the car, reviewing the steps to be taken.

"Now dig, Benny . . . I'm tellin' you out front . . . don't even *think* about firin' on nobody unless they try to grab you. Okay?"

"Hey, bruh . . . I hear ya. I don't need no murder rap on me neither. I hear ya."

After fifteen minutes, and a last hit on the roaches they held between thumb and forefinger, they stepped out into the warm night air of the Westside, loaded.

Benny pulled out a scrap of paper and squinted at the address written on it under a street light. "It's in the middle of the block here."

Elijah checked the neighborhood out closely. One of those mixed dwelling kind of places . . . stacked shelves of people next to one owner dwellings.

Elijah nodded to Benny as they paused in front of the

target, slid up the passageway leading to the back door and listened. The unmistakeable sound of a black gambling scene played itself out to them. Men grumblin', gamblin' and bettin'. They smiled to each other as they adjusted handkerchiefs over their noses.

Elijah removed the towel from the sawed-off shotgun, Benny pulled out his luger.

Benny tapped on the door with just the right amount of force, it would never do to have the gamblers think that they were the police.

"Yeah?" a voice asked from inside.

"Me, Sam," Elijah slurred, knowing out front that they had to know a Sam, from somewhere.

They brushed past the doorman and stood with their backs to the door.

"Awright, everybody, freeze! Don't move another muscle!"

One of the eight men standing around the table turned with a cynical look on his face. "Man, c'mon on! you got t' be jivin'!"

By previous agreement Benny skipped over to the speaker and slapped him across the face with his luger. The other men understood now, that it was a gambling house robbery, probably by dope fiends, which meant they couldn't be monkeyin' around. They snatched their respective piles of money from the table and stood with their hands raised.

Elijah took an indecisive step toward the group with his piece at shoulder level, uncertain as to whether he should make them keep their hands on the table because he had said, don't move another muscle, or whether or not he should make them keep their hands in the air.

The tension was wiping his high away and making him feel higher at the same time. He mopped sweat from his brow.

"Everybody! kneel! faces to the floor! asses in the air!" he heard himself say loudly. Good! We can deal with them better on the floor.

Benny looked at him gratefully. There was something very intimidating about being in a dingy, smoked-filled room with a bunch of big ol' thug ass niggers, sweating bullets over a jiveass robbery.

One of the gamblers, a big, butter-necked dope peddler, pinky ring flashing, even in the dull light, grumbled, "Looka here, blood . . . you gon' make me get my suit all messed up."

Elijah, on his job, knowing that all challenges had to be met and dealt with, if they hoped to survive, spoke coldly. "If you don't get your ass up in the air super quick, that ain't all you gon' get messed up!"

The utter seriousness of his tone, the shotgun and Benny efficiently snatching money away from hands, out of pockets and wherever else it could be found, confirmed the unspoken, dope fiend thing about them.

A nationalist in the bunch, terribly pissed, couldn't resist the urge to speak out against an outrage. "Y'all sho' is some cold-blooded motherfuckers! robbin' yo' own people!"

Benny kicked at the crack of his ass as hard as he could and almost fell.

Elijah spotted the toilet door on the other side of the room and almost fainted. What if there had been someone in the shithouse!

Being extra careful not to call Benny by name, he asked, "You got it all?"

Benny nodded, trying to pull the fat gambler's pinky ring off. The man offered no resistance and no aid.

Elijah allowed Benny a few pulls before beckoning for him to give it up. Diamond rings were worth a lot of bread sometimes.

"Awright! everybody in the shithouse! One at a time!"

Several of the men started to rise.

"Down! crawl!" Elijah poked his piece into several rib cages, being unnecessarily brutal in order to make his point.

Once again, he felt like fainting when he realized that they had not searched anyone, and that every one of the dudes crawling into the toilet might have a piece on him.

"Search 'em before they crawl in, man!" he called out to Benny.

Benny looked at him hatefully, for a quick moment. Why did he have to continue taking the dangerous chances involved with being close to these dudes, running the risk of being grabbed. He slapped out at a stray head, maintaining his brutality image as he haphazardly patted here and there on the men crawling past him.

"Hey, man . . . we can't all crawl into the shithouse, we got to stand up in order to get in here."

Elijah motioned for the men rising up to stay down. "Crawl up on top of each other, don't stand up!"

The last four men crawled in over the backs of the others, mad, disgusted. When the last man had crawled in, Elijah stuffed a nearby chair under the knob. "That oughta hold 'em for a few minutes."

They could hear the grumbling grow louder and louder as they moved to the door. A soft knock stopped them in their tracks.

The knock came again, a bit more urgently.

"Yeah?" Benny asked, creeping up to the door.

"Joe Mason and Clifford."

He looked at the toilet doorknob twisting and popping against the back of the chair. *Too bad I can't fire a round at them motherfuckers.*

The two men, realizing that they had the advantage because they knew what was going down, nodded to each other with complete understanding.

Benny jerked the door open. Elijah cocked his piece on them. "Awright, goddamn you! c'mon in! quick!"

The two men strolled in, disgusted expressions stamped all over their faces. Benny took their money off of them, stuffed it into his pockets with all the rest and pushed them down to the floor. "Make one move 'n it's your ass!" he told them and kicked one of the men in the ribs for emphasis.

They shot through the door, realizing that it was a run for their asses now, mainly because it was, and because the dudes who had just come in were going to open the cage of tigers in the toilet the minute they were out of sight.

Running behind Benny through the narrow passageway to the street, Elijah had the sudden, sinking feeling that they had lost, that the gamblers were going to catch them and grind their asses under heel.

They hit the street, running, Elijah realized after a few quick steps, the wrong way.

"Benny! Benny!" he called out, disregarding a group of people lounging around on their front stoop. "Benny! the cars the other way!"

Benny looked around at Elijah, surprised and scared, realized that he was right and started back in the other direction with him. They raced past the gambling house just as the first of the gamblers were starting out. Elijah fired a round from the shotgun into the air, intimidating the first pursuers. And kept on steppin'.

By unspoken agreement, they decided not to head for the car, to give their getaway vehicle away . . . instead they raced into the first alley they came to.

Pausing under a porch light for breath, Elijah looked at Benny's sweat-soaked face and laughed. "Li'l bit outta shape, huh?"

Benny nodded yes, gasping for breath.

The close sound of a bunch of men talking started them off again, trying to do a big circle and make it back to the car. They hopped over a fence and into someone's back yard, complete with a huge German shepherd on a chain. The three of them froze for a full ten seconds, the animal's ears peaked up for this unusual intrusion.

The dog made his lunge at Benny, already scrambling back over the fence, screaming.

Elijah dropped over beside him, dealing with the awkward shotgun carefully.

"You awright, man?"

Benny whimpered like a baby and stood up to feel his behind. "Yeah, yeah . . . I'm okay, I thought he had ripped a hole in my ass for a minute, it's just my pants."

The dog, not content to chase them out of his yard, began to woof at them from the other side of the fence.

"Who that down there?" a heavy male voice called from the shadows of one of the porches.

They trotted to the back gate, peeked out cautiously and continued their trip through the alley.

Trying to take a short cut through what looked like a small parking lot caused them both to trip over a low slung chair, draped across the entrance. Both men sprawled, moaning from the pain crackling up from their shins . . . the chase momentarily forgotten. Benny recovered first and, with deep compassion, helped Elijah to his feet. "C'mon, bruh . . . we can't lay here moanin' all night, we got to get to my ride."

They hobbled off, groaning a bit from the pain, in deep trouble now, because most of the neighborhood, in its own hip, telepathic way, was aware that someone had robbed the gambling joint.

Elijah spotted them first and nudged Benny. Three men searching through the alley, coming toward them. Realizing they couldn't run away without exposing themselves, they eased up into the deep shadows of someone's back porch.

The noises of a party coming to their ears from the second floor made both of them feel naked, as though the men searching for them would automatically look underneath the party noises.

The squad car popped through from the other end of the alley, catching the three men squarely in its spotlight as they met, practically in front of Elijah and Benny's hiding place. Both of them tried to become invisible.

The two white men in the squad car, taking no chances in the ghetto, kept the three men in the light of their car as they leaned out, pistols drawn, and asked questions.

"What's going on here?" the most aggressive one asked. "We got a report of a shooting."

"Ain't no shootin' here, officer. Musta been a false call," one of the men answered, the "right" tone of voice for rookie pigs carrying over into the shadows.

Elijah and Benny smiled.

"What're you guys doing out here in the alley?" the other cop asked.

"We lives out here . . . in the alley," a sarcastic voice answered.

"Don't be funny with us, fella. Just answer the goddamned question!"

"Awww, he was just jivin', officer," the first voice eased in, cooling the white boy out. "We on our way home from a stag show."

The irritation that rang out in the cop's voice said many things. Mainly, I'd give anything to blow one of you bastards away. "Okay! okay! enough of this bullshit! Let's clear this alley! Move it!"

The three men, into their neighborhood in a way that the white men could never be, faded away into familiar passageways, disappearing for the period of time it would take the squad car to find something else to do.

Elijah tried to ease his squatting position into something more comfortable. Sweat slithered down the sides of Benny's face.

The men eased out of the shadows as soon as the car

drove away and regrouped in the center of the alley to discuss what to do.

"Dig, Jack, why don't you 'n Nate get your car and wheel around a bit? They still 'round here somewhere. Melvin, Carson and J.D. went home for they pieces. We gon' find these rotten motherfuckers tonight."

A couple party goers, half juiced, flowed out onto the porch and leaned over the bannisters.

"What's happenin' down there!? Whatch'all doin'? playin' in the garbage cans? hahh hahh hah."

One of the searchers threw an empty can, half in play, half seriously, up at the drunk.

"Mind yo' own business, asshole! 'n leave ours alone."

They waited for a few minutes, to allow the searchers to go on, before risking a few words.

"Lead pipe cinch my ass!" Elijah growled at Benny.

Benny, stuffed in a corner behind an old sofa, shrugged eloquently. They both maintained their positions . . . tired, hurt, aching, afraid.

"Heyyy, Benny . . . I got an idea, take off your coat 'n hat . . . we're goin' upstairs to a party."

Benny stared across the distance between them, not believing his ears. "Mannnnn, have you gone in-sane?"

Elijah decided not to argue. He stood and took off his hip bush jacket, wrapped the broken down shotgun in it.

"This ain't registered, is it?"

"Hell no! but . . . ohh, I see, I see what you doin'. Yeahhh!" In order not to make their stuff look hidden, arousing someone's suspicions maybe, before they could get back to it, they crushed the wrapped-up shotgun and

Benny's luger into a jumbled heap on the sofa, along with a pile of other rags, and eased up the stairs to the party.

"Hey, 'Lijah," Benny whispered at the top of the stairs, "I got a rip in my pants, man."

"You still got your ass, ain't you?" The two men eased into the back door into the kitchen, fending off the hostile stares of a few dudes lounging around who saw competition for the home stretch.

A tall, well-assembled woman stood behind a table loaded with fried chicken, wrinkles, potato salad, monkey bread, cole slaw, bean pies . . . a soul food smorgasbord, one fist mounted on a lush hip, a drink in the other.

"Awright people! let's buy some of these dinners! Me 'n Shirley didn't spend all day cleanin' these wrinkles for our health!"

Elijah moved obliquely over to the table, Benny scuttling along close to him, trying to conceal the rip in his pants.

"Uhh, I'd like a dinner, sister."

She smiled at him warmly, and at the sudden line that developed behind him. She set her drink down and began to pile food onto a paper plate for Elijah.

"Somebody'll be taking my place in a few minutes," she mumbled, her eyes boldly meeting Elijah's for a few seconds, "and I'll be ready to dance."

He paid for the dinner and stepped away with a grin on his face, liking the down home flavor of the place, the music coming from the front, the food and the woman serving it.

"How is it, man?" Benny asked, pointing at the food with his nose.

"Why don't you buy a dinner 'n see?" Elijah teased him, drifting up a long hall to the source of the music, strobe lights flickering over a bunch of Westside black folks doin' the Funky Notion.

He stood off to the side, Benny so close to his right arm that he had to take a step away from him to raise his hand to his mouth.

"Man, how can you be standin' up here eatin', at a time like this?"

Elijah frowned at Benny, gnawed on a chicken bone for a bit, wondering about it himself, and replied, "The main reason I can be standin' up here eatin', at a time like this, is 'cause I'm hungry as a motherfucker."

A few of the tense lines on Benny's forehead relaxed. "'Lijah, you somethin' else!"

Elijah nodded graciously in Benny's direction, polishing off the food in huge, nervous mouthfuls.

What sense did it make to stay tense? he asked himself, knowing that there was no money in that, no groove, nothing.

He pinpointed three black Earthmothers, each of them with comfortable shelves underneath the mold of their fleshy bottoms, stomping and twisting their bodies to the beat. God! black women sho' have got beautiful asses!

Yeahhh, what sense did it make to be all up tight . . . ? Despite the fact that they were "wanted" . . . not by some civilized law enforcement agency, but by a bunch of dudes who wanted to give them the kind of ass kickin' that would put them both in the hospital for a while. Or the morgue.

The good flavor of the food suddenly evaporated with

the thought. "Benny, you want the rest o' this?"

"Thought you was so hungry?"

"I was, before Miss Lady popped in."

He handed the plate to Benny and held his arms out to Mabel Stewart. She smiled at his gesture, both of them glad that it was a slow number for their first dance together.

The mingling of perfumes, perspiration, the smoke, music and the flickering light pushed them closer together, established a moment. Elijah slid his hand down to her lower back, testing.

She protested by nibbling on his right earlobe. The music played on. And on . . . soul sounds to grind by, and ended too soon.

They stood toe to toe at the end of the record, feeling excited about each other. "Feelin' as good as you feel to me, you could tell me your name, to begin with."

"Mabel. Mabel Stewart, what's yours?"

Elijah quickly ran through all the reasons why he should not give his right name, reasoned out that there was no need to lie. "Uhhh, Elijah Brookes, the first."

"Tell me somethin', Elijah Brookes, the first?"

"Anything you righteously want to know, baby," he macked to her.

"Why is your friend over there at the window? peeking out like that. You'd swear somebody was after him or somethin'."

Elijah looked at her closely, realized that she was trying to tell him something. " 'Scuse me a minute."

He made his way through the people jammed up on the dance floor, waiting for the next record to start.

"Looka here, brotherman . . ."

Benny almost dropped the plate as he turned away from the window.

"Ohh, 'Lijah . . . you scared me, man . . . I thought . . ."

"Yeah, I know. Dig, I thought I'd hip you to the fact that most of the people here know that the gamblin' joint down the street's been ripped off" . . . he leaned closer, speaking out of the corner of his mouth, "and it wouldn't take too many more suspicious moves outta your shaky ass to give us away."

Benny's shaking hand dropped the plate, splattering chicken bones at Elijah's feet.

Elijah looked down disdainfully as he scrambled to put the food back on the plate. What the hell ever made him go out on a sting with Benny? Greed, he answered himself.

Benny stood up, hating the look in Elijah's eyes.

"Look, 'Lijah, I been checkin' out the scene down on the street . . . these dudes is fo' real, they got regular patrols 'n shit out. How we gon' get outta this?"

"Well, tell you what." He shot a full smile across the room at Mabel. "The first thing we gon' have to do is split up . . ."

Benny glanced enviously at Mabel.

"You done got yourself into somethin', huh?"

"Maybe . . . at any rate, let's split the bread, just in case."

The music started, blaring out Benny's answer.

Elijah pulled him across the room, thinking, on second thought, that it would be better to go off and take care business in a private place.

"You know how to move faster than a two step?" Mabel

asked him as the two men approached her.

"Hey, lady . . . I was raised up dancin', but lemme take a rain check for this one, where is the li'l room?"

She pointed down the hall, slightly pissed that he wasn't dancing every dance with her.

Benny stood in the center of the toilet, looking pitiful.

"Well. C'mon, man . . . I don't want to hang out in the shithouse all night."

Benny, looking more pitiful every second, dug down in his pockets and pulled out a bunch of one-dollar bills. "I . . . uhh . . . I . . . this is all I got on me."

"Fuck, you mean, this is all you got on you, where's the rest?"

Benny pressed his chin down to his chest, looking, for all the world like a five-year-old caught with his hand in the jam pot. "I stuffed it in my coat pockets, all the rest of it, it's down on the porch."

Elijah turned a cold, hard, mean look on him, half a beat away from sticking boot to him. "Okay, let's divide what we got here and go downstairs."

Benny carefully divided the forty-six dollars he had.

Elijah looked at the money as though it had funky mold on it. Twenty-three fuckin' dollars for risking his life.

He grabbed Benny by the collar. "Is this all?"

"That's it, bruh . . . I mighta dropped a li'l taste, jumpin' over fences 'n stuff, but this is it."

"What possessed you to leave the bread in your god-damned coat pocket?" Elijah asked, more in anguish than anger.

"You told me to leave my coat, man! You told me!

55

remember?!"

"I didn't tell you to leave the dough in it! C'mon on! Let's go git it!"

He ignored the curious stares of the two women waiting to get into the toilet. No time for any off-brand bullshit.

Mable stared at the backs of the two men, making their way, super-casually, it seemed at first glance, back to the kitchen. She followed at a discreet distance, determined not to lose Elijah, no matter what. Not this Saturday night, at any rate.

Benny and Elijah stood on the back porch, smoking cigarettes and looking up and down the dark alley below, trying to conceal their anxiety.

Mabel offered the sister selling food a hand, surreptitiously checking out the two men framed in the light spilling out onto the porch.

She wandered out onto the porch as they slipped down the porch steps. Was he trying to sneak off? Wowwww . . . I must really be losing my touch.

Elijah and Benny crouched in the darkness at the bend of the porch steps, halted by the sight of a couple slumped down on the sofa, cooing and caressing each other.

Elijah felt like spitting with disgust. Benny simply stared, intensely interested at the sight of the woman's hand inside the man's fly, and his hand under her dress.

Mable quickly returned to the kitchen as they quietly trudged back up the stairs.

"Well, it's all safe for a while, I guess," Elijah whispered, mad *and* disgusted, "unless they decide to push every goddamned thing off the sofa."

"Nawww, they won't do that, be more likely that they would be layin' up on stuff."

"I hope you right, Benny. I sure hope you're right, for your sake."

Mabel met Elijah as they re-entered the kitchen with a drink, ignoring Benny. "Here, here's one on the house. What's the problem? You look like somebody just stole your last dime."

Elijah cut a mean look at Benny. "Somebody did, in a way."

"Well, hey, let's not let bad vibes spoil a good party."

Elijah took a long sip on the water glass and smiled at Mabel, in spite of his mood.

"Where you from, Mabel?"

"I'm from Chittlin' Switch, Miss'ssippi, honey, and we don't be jivin' when it comes to havin' a good time."

She grabbed Elijah's hand and gently tugged him back through the hall, to the dance floor, her sense of power restored.

CHAPTER 3

Elijah was startled to see the streaks of daylight filter in through the front window. He looked over Mabel's shoulder at the dregs of a party, people slopped over chairs, beer cans everywhere, stale cigarette smoke in the air, the music down into a mellow jazz groove now, James Brown and Aretha played out. Benny sound asleep on an overstuffed chair.

He released his grip on Mabel's waist and held her back from him, to check her out in the morning light . . . the acid test.

She leaned back against the wall, completely aware of what he was doing. "Thirty-eight, thirty-eight, twenty-five, thirty-eight," she recited in a detached voice, "and the circles are from stayin' up with you all night."

They both laughed, in tune with each other, and fell

back into each other's arms.

"Like I told you, baby, earlier, I'm a Cancer man and we like to be sure that the feelin' is there before we give ourselves away."

"Well, is it there?" she asked seriously.

"Uhh huh," he answered without hesitation, and then suddenly remembered. "'Scuse me a minute, baby."

He went over and shook Benny awake. "Benny! Benny! Wake up! Benny!"

Mabel looked at the two of them curiously as Elijah whispered urgently into Benny's ear. "You been back downstairs?"

Benny yawned and blinked, trying to get himself together. "Downstairs? downstairs? what downstairs? Oohh, nawww, I ain't been . . ."

Elijah resisted the urge to crack him in the jaw, moved quickly through the hall, to the back door and down the steps to the sofa. "Well, I'll be a sonovabitch!" he cursed aloud, staring at the sofa, cleared now of the rags that had been there, of their coats, guns, and the money. "Well, I'll be a sonovabitch!"

"What's wrong? You lose somethin' down there?" Mabel asked from the top of the stairs, Benny hanging back behind her sheepishly.

He jammed both hands into his pockets to keep from strangling Benny and mumbled, "Nawww, not really . . . not really."

Mabel decided not to press the matter, knowing that he was not about to give her the straight of things at this point. "Uhh, Elijah, did you say you were goin' to give me a lift home?"

Elijah glared fiercely at Benny, answering Mabel. "Yeah, baby . . . we're takin' you home. You got the keys to the car, Benny?"

Benny dug down into his pocket and pulled his keys out. "I always carry 'em in my pants pocket."

Mabel looked from Benny's petulant, sheepish-li'l-boy-done-wrong expression to Elijah's scowl and put it all together.

"Hold on a second, you guys . . . I got to say somethin' to Stella before I split."

The two men stood at the front door waiting for Mabel to say a few parting words to her girlfriend.

"'Lijah, I'm really sorry, man . . . really I am."

Elijah studied Benny's contrite expression, decided to forgive him, a little bit. "Yeahhh, well, that's the way it goes down sometimes."

Down on the early Sunday morning streets, Mabel linked her arms through theirs and asked, just as they were walking past the gambling joint on rubber legs, "Y'all held up the gamblin' joint last night, didn't you?"

Benny's arm stiffened.

"Uhh huh," Elijah answered, "and then we got robbed by the robbers . . . I guess."

Benny fumbled with the keys trying to open the car door. "Where we goin'?" he asked slyly, as they positioned themselves in the car . . . single man driving, the couple being chauffeured.

Elijah and Mabel exchanged warm looks in the back seat.

"Four-three-seven-nine Warren Boulevard," she answered

after a slight, polite, pregnant pause.

Benny sheeled through the Sunday morning streets, glancing from Elijah and Mabel kissing in the rear-view mirror to sedate groups of churchgoers, off to seek salvation.

He slid into a space almost in front of Mabel's address, a canopied, third-rate, third-class, rundown hotel tenement.

"Awright folks, here we be."

He waited, diplomatically, to see whether or not Elijah was going to go in with his new-found friend. When it was obvious that he was going to, he asked, "Whatchu want me to do, man . . . pick you up later?"

Mabel, on firm ground now, having caught, called out across the pavement, "What's this 'later' shit? You can pick 'im up in the mornin' . . . if he wants you to."

"Uhh . . . yeah, man . . . why don't you pick me up in the mornin'?"

Benny shrugged behind the wheel. "That's cool with me, what time?"

"I go to work at eight," she answered promptly.

"I hear ya, baby . . . I hear ya!" Benny sang out as he screeched away from the curb, happy to have survived the night.

Elijah and Mabel shuffled up the dim, smelly steps to the third floor, each of them quietly excited by the idea of what was about to happen, old pros at it, but still enthusiastic.

He stood close behind her as she unlocked the door, curious as to how they would pull it off, how they would get it on.

She strolled into the apartment, made a sweeping gesture that said, "Well, here it is," and pointed to the toilet.

"You can use that blue toothbrush, it's never been used before," she said to him, implications dangling in several directions.

Elijah brushed his teeth and impulsively decided to shower. He stood under the warm jet, trying to make something out of what was about to happen, but couldn't. It was simply another piece of ass. Another piece of ass. Another piece of ass.

He stared down at the slow, throbbing erection the hot water had given him, wishing, in a way that he were at home, in his own place, with Leelah.

"You constipated, baby?" Mabel called through the door, a laugh in her voice.

Elijah forced himself to laugh back as he answered, "Nawwww, it's just that when you got the claps, it's hard to pee."

He shut off the water to listen to Mabel's laughter. She really is a sho' 'nuff, down to earth, stone soul to the bone bitch.

She was still laughing, sprawled across her bed, when he popped out of the bathroom, a towel saronged around his waist.

He dived on top of her gently, feeling sleepy, playful and giddy because of it.

"Wait a minute!" she squirmed out from underneath him. "I have to take this tampon out."

It was his turn to crack up as she went for her shower. So groovy to come across a deep sister with a sense of humor.

He listened patiently to all of her movements removing

her make-up . . . the shower, the cleansing of the face, the clatter of jar tops, the cologne spray . . .

She stood nude in the doorway of the bedroom, showing him that her body was still firm after thirty-eight years of living and asked, seriously, "Elijah, you don't have v.d. for real, do you?"

His impulse was to say no, but he canceled it out, why spoil the fun so soon?

He pulled the corner of the cover back for her to get in bed with him.

"Ain't but one way to find out," he said, using her serious tone.

She hesitated for a full ten seconds before sliding under the covers with him.

"You a devil, you know that?" she whispered before he kissed her.

"I know . . . I know I am . . ."

Mabel, in her starched white nurse's uniform, sat on the side of the bed, gently shaking Elijah awake, a smile on her face. "Elijah! Elijah! . . . I'm goin'. There's some sausage 'n eggs in the fridge and I made some orange juice for you."

He stifled a yawn, turning to face her. "What time will you be home?"

"Ohhh, 'bout five-thirty, six."

He folded her into his arms, pecking little thank-you-for-yesterday-and-last-night kisses on her face. "I'll call you this evenin'."

"You don't have to jive me, baby . . . Momma's fo' real."

"I know you are. I'm not jivin', I *will* call."

Mabel pulled back. "Okay, if you do, you do. I won't be disappointed if you don't."

"I heard my old man put that together once, a long time ago, in a different way ... 'expect,' he said, 'at most, nothin', and ye shall, at least, not be too damned disappointed.'"

"Your ol' man sounds like a wise dude."

Elijah played with the buttons on her uniform. "He was," he replied, and traced a love trail with his finger tips along the side of her neck, trickled off into her ears for a bit.

Mabel, responding positively to his vibes, pulled gently at his nipple tips.

It had been a tender, beautiful experience ... they said with their eyes, and their practiced, gentle touches. A tender, complete, beautiful experience. All of the right chemicals, the right feelings, beautiful.

Elijah reached out for her again, a more serious hug on his mind this time. "I gotta go!" Mabel screamed playfully, wanting to jump back in bed with him. "I gotta go! with all these bills 'n things I got, I can't afford to ... call me this evenin'? okay?"

Elijah lay back, cooling himself out. "I said I would."

She blew him a kiss and was off to her job.

He pursed his lips, looking up into the ceiling, and scratched through his pubic hairs with long indulgent strokes. Life sho' was beautiful at times. He scratched and flashed back through the events that led up to Mabel.

Yesterday. Only yesterday? he frowned at the thought. Sometimes the shit moved too quickly, took in too much. Doin' the short change scene with the Geech, the grabbing, back to the pad, knocking off a li'l piece with Leelah ...

64

opps, forgot about Dee Dee. Sorry 'bout that, Dee Dee girl. Making the set at the Tiger, off with Benny.

He gritted his back teeth together. Benny the Bone, chickenshit, lame . . . oh well, what the hell, we got away with our asses still split down the middle, instead of cracks slashed crosswise.

He felt his rumbling belly and let out a long, low fart. Wonder what those motherfuckers would've done if they'd caught us? He smiled at the idea of being caught. Sounds like a war game or something. No doubt what they would've done . . . after they had broken both our legs for openers.

The party . . . and Mabel. His mind telescoped itself back to the moment. Mabel Stewart. He looked around the apartment. A little larger than his own. Nothing in it that was worth too much.

How many apartments like this have I woke up in? he asked himself. The memories of some of them made him smile. The "bohemian" white bitch who had rented an apartment in the ghetto, in order to secure a ready supply of black dick. The twenty-two-year-old sister from Washington, D.C. . . . . off into her own bag for the first time. The nymphomaniac with the foul breath and slack titties. The factory worker from Memphis who thought that her crummy little apartment was outta sight because, for the first time in her life, she was not sleeping all squeezed up with four other brothers 'n sisters.

He unconsciously shook his head, looking for some new patterns of thought. It never paid to hang too far back in the past for too long, that's the way a lot of dudes became stagnant. Mabel Stewart . . . nice, kind of clinger, but what could you expect from a broad thirty-eight years old?

He whipped the covers off, remembering the sausage and eggs she'd reminded him she had. Standing up and stretching, his eye was caught by a trio of brown envelopes sticking up behind a jewelry box on the dresser. He picked them up, read the titles lettered on each one. "Sears," "Rent," "Food," peeked inside and counted a total of two hundred and fifty dollars.

He slowly replaced the envelopes and headed for the toilet. Eight-thirty, time to start the day off. Benny would be coming through in a bit, making excuses for himself and telling lies.

He wolfed down four eggs, four sausages, drank coffee and dressed carefully.

Gotta change clothes soon as I get home, he thought, sniffing the armpits of his shirt.

The doorbell ringing caught him off balance. Who could it be? One of Mabel's man friends, sneaking by to try for a li'l piece of wake-me-up?

"Yeah?" he called into the intercom.

"Me, Benny," a nazalized voice replied.

He buzzed him in and waited, standing in the center of the front room. Time to get back onto the track.

"Heyyy, man, I hope I didn't hang you up or nothin' by takin' so long, but what happened was . . ."

"Skip it, blood . . . I didn't expect you here 'til 'bout this time anyway."

Benny quickly slid away from the rest of the alibis and excuses he had prepared, unnecessarily. "You ready to go?" he asked.

"Yeah, let's cut out."

He opened the door for Benny and started out after him. "Hold on a minute, Benny."

He walked back to the bedroom and took the money out of the envelopes and stuffed it into his pocket. What the fuck! they'd never see each other again anyway.

He looked up into Benny's face, grinning at him from the front room. He decided not to make any comment about his actions. The less said, the better. "C'mon, let's git on."

Benny bounced down the steps behind him, proud to be given the chance to hang out, if only for a little while, with, next to himself, one of the rottenest motherfuckers on the Southside.

Elijah slumped down in the seat next to Benny, feeling tired, despite the fact that he had been in bed for a whole day and all night.

Monday morning, ten-thirty, hot already. He looked out at the people in the corridor between the Westside and the Southside, the black folks who were not off to spend their day doing the white boy's work . . . the too old, the too young, the too lame, the too hip. Made matters very simple for the police . . . if you were on the street doing anything, anything at all, it was very likely that you might be stopped, searched, incarcerated, just like that. Simply because you were black, in the ghetto, and likely to be doing something illegal for those very reasons.

Benny paused at an intersection to allow five young brothers to cross the street. Obviously lacking anything else to do, they hung traffic up by stopping in the middle of the street so that two of their number could stage an impromptu karate exhibition.

Taking their time, they went through a series of violent movements. Benny sat patiently, whispering to Elijah out of the corner of his mouth, "Look at these assholes, blockin' traffic with they bullshit!"

Elijah said nothing, simply looked at all of the vitality and energy being wasted in the middle of the street.

Finally, drifting on, the gang members contemptuously released the traffic flow, satisfied with their show of strength. Elijah saluted them with a raised fist. They looked at his move scornfully . . . an older dude trying to be hip, into their thang. He slowly lowered his fist, feeling slightly put down, but understanding.

Yeahhh, it is a different scene, it's your scene now, li'l brothers, I sure in fuck hope y'all do a lot better with it than we did.

He eased out of the car in front of his apartment, anxious to shave, shower again, change clothes and take care business . . . it helped to have two hundred and fifty dollars to start the day off with too.

He slammed the car door and leaned back in the window to lay a sarcastic parting shot on Benny. "Looka here, dog nuts . . . the next time you get ready to go stick somebody up, be sure 'n come get me, okay?"

Benny hung his head a little. "Awwww, well, you know how it goes sometimes, man."

"Yeah, brother," Elijah replied, a more sympathetic tone in his voice. "Yeahhh, I know how it is. What comes around, goes around."

Benny shrugged and pulled away slowly, knowing that it would be most unlikely that he and Elijah would be getting together to do anything, ever again.

Elijah, off onto other motions, spent the two hundred and fifty bucks on his way up to the apartment he shared with Leelah, whenever the both of them were there together. Replaced the two hundred and fifty seconds before he opened the door with four hundred and something he would get, somehow.

He glided into the apartment, expecting to go through a little lightweight number with Leelah. Almost in a state of shock, he closed the door; where were the clock radios, the six two-hundred-dollar suits, the two portable color television sets? and Leelah? where was Leelah?

He stumbled across the room to the dresser, to the small wooden box with the wristwatches in it. He fingered through them. All of the expensive ones were gone.

He rushed over to the closet to check on his own personal wardrobe. Nothing missing. He sat on the side of the bed and thought it out carefully. That dirty, dirty rotten bitch! She had taken all of the shit he had fenced from the dope fiends and made off. Dirty rotten punk bitch!

Tears swelled up in his eyes at the thought of her betrayal. It wasn't so bad that she had split . . . but to have taken all of his shit too. That was too much.

He sat, staring into space, for a few long minutes. His main lady, the one who was going to not only see him living on a hill, but the one who was going to help him get there. The bitch was gone . . . He stood up stiffly and walked over to his closet for a change of clothing.

Draping a dark ensemble on his body as an indication of his murky mood, he stood in front of the cracked mirror mounted over the dresser. Could you ever trust any bitch? he asked the image buttoning his shirt with wooden fingers. Could you ever trust any bitch, fo' real?

He felt vaguely like crying but he hadn't done that in such a long time that he wasn't certain if his bad vibes contained tears or not.

What should I do? he formed the words carefully in the mirror. What should I do? he almost spelled the words out to himself. Get drunk! his image said to him, and winked.

"Goddamned right!" he spoke aloud to himself and decided on the spot, at eleven-fifteen in the morning, Monday, July twelfth, to get sloppy pissy drunk.

"The bitch done cut out on me," he mumbled once more, on the way out, two hundred and fifty easy pieces burning a hole in his pocket.

Downstairs, on the street, he paused in front of his apartment building, looking up one side of the street and down the other, both fists on his narrow hips, wishing that he could spot Leelah somewhere.

Walking south on Prairie, toward 47th Street, he somehow had the feeling that everybody on the street, even the old people hanging out on their porches knew about his woman's desertion.

Turning the corner on 47th, heading for the Tip Tap Lounge, he spotted Leelah's best friend and sometimes lover (whenever her love came down on her that way), Zelma Mercer.

"Hey Zelma!" he yelled across the street, untypical of him, and dodged some afternoon traffic to skip across to her.

Zelma, a firmly built lesbian person with a permanent scowl and a profound disgust for trifling niggers, like the one skipping over to her, glared at Elijah's approach.

"Zelma, you seen Leelah?" he asked breathlessly, trying to conceal his anxiety.

She showed her teeth to him in a caricature of a smile. "Yeahhh, I saw her, earlier."

Elijah resisted the urge to throw a shot at her jaw. Never could tell, not with a bitch that looked strong as Zelma, and it would be terrible to get your ass kicked on the street . . . even if it was by a bulldagger . . . like, well, after all, she was still a woman.

He decided to spool out honey rather than spit vinegar. "Uhhh, how long ago? She asked me to cop a half a piece for her and I did, now I can't find her. And if I don't find her soon, I'm gon' have to do it myself . . . hahh hahhhah."

Zelma, realizing that what Leelah had, Zelma could get some of . . . and she loved girl . . . blurted out, "I saw her a few hours ago, I heard her ask Mickey Mouse to give her a ride out to the airport."

Elijah's jaw slopped down. "The airport! what airport?"

"The main one," Zelma answered heavily, and kept on stepping.

Elijah stood, rooted to the spot, watching Zelma's roly-poly shuffle, sweat streaming down the sides of his face. The airport . . . guess she must've decided to go on back to the Coast, to 'Frisco. "Come on, Elijah, let's pack up 'n get on out to the Coast, you'd love San Francisco. Not only that, things are a helluva lot easier out there."

He slung the corners of his mouth down, feeling rejected, disgusted, sad, hurt, mad, and walked the twenty-five steps to the first bar.

For the rest of the day, during the heat of the middle of the day, and into the early cool breezes off of the lake, he slowly made his way through the bars in the neighborhood. First on one side of the street and then the other, hoping, on one hand, that the Lord, or whoever was responsible, would return his bottom woman. And, on the other hand, that he could get drunk.

By the time he reached the Tiger Lounge, having saved it for last, he had guzzled and swizzled his way through eight beers and fourteen gin 'n tonics and felt sober as a black Presbyterian preacher. He sat at the bar, trying to decide whether or not he should have two double shots of Jack and probably get sick, spilling it in on top of the beer and gin 'n tonics, or continue with the gin.

"You want me to come back to you, brotherman?" Sly Bob the bartender asked, checking Elijah's melancholy state out with a seasoned eye.

"Huh?"

"You want me to . . . ?"

"Ohh, uhhh, lemme have a double gin 'n tonic."

Sly Bob swabbed the place in front of Elijah with a couple quick flicks of his wrist. "A double gin 'n tonic, huh?" he repeated the request as a semi-question.

"Yeahhh, a double gin 'n tonic."

Elijah looked over the assembled slicksters from the bar,

nodding casually to the people he knew, ignoring those he didn't know. He lushed the double down in four swallows, paid the tab, and stumbled off the stool and out of the door, fucked up at last.

"Mannnn," one of the regulars leaned across the bar to comment to Sly Bob. "What's happenin' with 'Lijah? I ain't never seen him to down like that."

Sly Bob watched Elijah bump into the side of the door frame on his way out. "Ain't no tellin' what's goin' down. Lotsa shit be happenin' secretly in a dude's life sometimes. Some shit be so deep that you can't do nothin' but weep 'n drink."

The regular, a player and a tender heart himself, reached over and slapped Bob's fat palm lightly.

"Right on, brother! righteous on!"

Elijah trudged up the dim steps to his apartment, stumbling from time to time, drunk, but still careful to keep his hand on his knife on the dark staircase.

For the second time he felt shock opening his door. Leelah lowered the confession magazine and held the joint she was smoking out to him.

"From the looks of you, I don't guess this would do anything to you," she said, and scooched her back up a little higher on the pillow.

Elijah reached behind him and missed the door with his first move, kicked it closed instead.

He did a little superstraight stutter step over to the high iron railing at the bottom of the bed.

He stood looking down at Leelah on the bed, her royal

blue robe slit open to the thigh, not sure of whether he wanted to strangle her or jump on top of her and start humping like a love-crazed Congolese gorilla.

"Leelah, where've you been and where is all my stuff?" he asked evenly, trying not to slur.

She laid the magazine on her stomach, took a long hit on the smoke and answered coldly, "You got mo' nerve than a brass-assed monkey, askin' me where *I've* been! That's what I oughta be askin' you!"

Elijah, seeing the dangers in trying to make something of the fact that they hadn't been in the same space for a couple days almost, decided to stay with more concrete questions. "Damn where anybody's been! What happened to all the stuff we had in here?"

"What the fuck do you think happened?"

Elijah started around the side of the bed, no longer shocked or puzzled, just angry now.

"Don't be playin' games with me, woman!" he snarled.

She smiled indulgently at his blustering behavior and sucked on the joint again before answering.

"Awwww, you know I sold that shit, 'Lijah. You don't have to stand there wolfin' at me. I ain't scared o' you, and you know it."

He took a couple deep breaths, cooling himself out, satisfied that they had it all back together again.

She passed the half-smoked tuskie to his outstretched fingers.

"Uhh, well, you know . . . I thought . . . I thought, with all the shit goin' on these days that maybe somebody had kidnapped you and ripped us off too."

Leelah's laughter shook the bed and forced tears out of her eyes. "Elijah! Elijah Brookes, the first! hahhh hahhh! hahhh! stop! please stop! hahhh hahhh hahhhaaahh! you 'bout fulla shit as a Christmas turkey!"

Elijah permitted himself a slight smile, realizing that she was right.

"How much we get? Browney take everything?"

"Yep, everything, for six bills."

He passed the roach to her with an incredulous look on his face. "Six bills!? Six suits was worth six bills."

"Well, actually I got seven," she purred at him, pushing the magazine off her stomach as she arched her back yawning, "but I bought a few things, and I copped a li'l taste for us. You want some?"

"Yeahh, yeah, I could dig some. Who'd you cop from?"

"Chink," she answered as she reached down under the side of the bed for her purse.

Elijah settled himself down on the side of the bed, the beers, gin 'n tonics, the heavy smoke and now, looking forward to the cocaine, he felt relaxed. Not to mention the release of tension he felt because his woman was back.

"Chink. Yeahhh, Chink usually has pretty nice shit."

Leelah took a couple medicine vials out of her purse and four hundred and fifty dollars in fifty-dollar bills. She counted the money out into Elijah's outstretched hand.

"Goddamn, Leelah baby! I thought you said we cleared six bills!"

She glared at him fiercely.

"Don't I get none of it? I mean, after all, I had to pay a couple dudes to take the shit outta here."

75

He frowned and jammed the money down his pocket. What could he say? knowing Leelah, more than likely she had probably gotten seven fifty. Sliced a hundred and half off the top for herself. Paid a hundred for the girl and nibbled fifty off to party with, or whatever. Slick bitch.

He watched her sprinkle a small mound of the white alkaloid powder on her compact mirror, divide it into four neat lines with the edge of a ten-dollar bill.

"I really thought you had cut out on me, baby. I really did."

She snorted up one line and down another before handing him the mirror, being careful to breath off to one side, so as not to blow any of the stuff away.

"What made you think a thing like that?"

Elijah snuffed up one line and down the other, his actions precise and well-ordered.

"Well, when I was worried about you today, lookin' everywhere . . . Zelma told me you had gone to the airport."

Leelah took the mirror and tapped a little more coke out onto it, dividing it once again into four straight lines.

Elijah, his nose turning to hot ice, stood unsteadily to take off his shirt.

"Nawwww, baby," she began slowly. "Momma was just out there takin' care business as usual. I thought it might be hip to stash the grab bag out there for a change, since you haven't done the airport for months."

He took the mirror and did two lines, handed it back to her.

"Yeahhh, well, I really got scared for a bit. I thought you had decided to make it on back to the Coast, to 'Frisco."

She snorted the last two lines up, licked the powdery residue from the mirror and dropped the compact and the bill into her purse.

Elijah settled himself beside her on the bed again, folded her up into his arms and felt like crying.

Leelah, stroking his neck and back, whispered into his ear, "How could I ever leave a motherfucker as rotten as you?"

He found himself, smiling over her shoulder despite the gentle insult, pushed her back onto the bed and stood up to take off the rest of his garments. What the hell! he rationalized, no one was paying him to be himself, they all wanted him to be someone else. Fuck 'em!

He slid back into Leelah's embrace under the cover.

"You know, that was really a dirty rotten thing for you to do?"

"What?" he asked, knowing already.

"You know, to leave me by myself in the Tiger the other night."

"Yeahhh, that sho' was rotten," he conceded after a moment's reflection, determined not to get caught in that bag again, and wrapped his naked thighs around hers.

CHAPTER 4

Elijah sat in the barber's chair, half asleep in the mid-day heat, digging on the scene around him.

Stacey, the seventy-year-old shoeshine "boy," popping his shine rag across a young brother's new platforms, the MOQ station beaming out jazz for sisters and brothers, a few early gambling men heading into the back room to get their third race bets down, Pauline the manicurist sitting in the window of the shop doing her own nails and flirting with the occasional, potential customer, Marvin, O.D. and Home cutting hair.

Elijah nodded cooperatively as Home chattered into his ear and snipped his Afro. "I don't care what y'all say . . . George Wallace is awright with me, at least you know where he is. What y'all thank about that, home?"

Elijah nodded, using his head to stay in tempo with

By Odie Hawkins

Home's monologue. He never really needed any consensus, just an audience . . . and with a barber's apron around a customer's neck, that's what he had.

"Now you take somebody like that li'l ol' rich boy from Massachusetts . . . what'shisname? the one with all the teeth 'n hair? Kangstiddy! yeahhh! Kangstiddy! that's the boy's name! lotsa folks thank he's for *us,* but it's really hard t' say, he ain't nothin' but a good politician, that's all he is, ain't that right, home?"

Elijah nodded on cue, his mind flirting with the idea of visiting Mabel. Or Dee Dee. Or maybe going to Detroit to play some funny cards at Mayburry's house.

"I bet you even dug Bilbo, didn't you, Home?" a middle-aged brother asked.

Home snipped a few stray ends from Elijah's head before answering. "Nawwww, naw, I didn't dig 'im. Not the way you mean, home."

Elijah opened his eyes. Who in the hell was Bilbo? who had he been? He searched around in his head to place the name. Ohhh yeahhh, the racist senator from Miss'ssippi, 1930s section.

"Well, if you didn't dig 'im," the brother pressed, "you was down there then, why didn't you rebel against 'im?"

Home screwed his lips down and snipped silently for a few naps, getting his retort together.

"Well, brotherman, since you really wanna know . . . one of the reasons why we didn't re-bel, one o' the reasons is that we was too busy reasonin' it all out, outsmartin' 'em, gittin' the thang together so that young bloods could git out in the streets 'n shoot that dope, kick sisters in the ass and have ol' motherfuckers like you ask dumb questions."

The barbershop suddenly seemed to be stricken with silence, despite the Coltrane's sounds sweeping out over the raidio and the noise of the streets flickering into the shop. Home?! was this Home being pissed off?! Wowwwww! but, once again, he re-discovered his good nature and whipped everything back into perspective. "Yeahhhh, that's what he is, Kangstiddy, a good goddamn politician, but then again, he just might really be sincere. Ain't no tellin' about a lotta these new white boys."

He finished Elijah's hair off with a final artistic snip, brushed his neck off and whipped the striped cover off with a flourish.

Elijah stood up, straightened his collar out, patted his hair narcissistically and laid a generous tip on Home.

Home stared at the extra dollar, realizing immediately what it meant. Like, hey . . . haircuts themselves cost too much. And a tip too!

"Certainly wants to thank you, home."

"Don't thank me, Home . . . thank that blue-eyed devil. He's the one who made it mean somethin' to you." Home stared up from the dollar tip to Elijah's cold expression, trying to put some meaning from it all into his feelings.

"Right on! home! right on!" he replied enthusiastically, not really understanding the undercurrent.

"Ohhh, and another thing," Elijah added, on his way out, "you can lump all them jiveass motherfuckers together, Republicans, Democrats, Communists, whatever . . . and if they white, they don't mean your black ass one bitta good."

"Sho' is cold, home! sho' is cold," Home sang out to one

of his favorite customers, still uncomprehending, but more in tune.

Elijah winked at Pauline on the way out and called back to Home. "It's a cold-blooded game, Home . . . a cold-blooded game."

Elijah stood in the entrance of the Stickhall, looking around, hat slashed to the side of his head, his nose a little bit in the air . . . shoes gleaming, pants creased straight through the bell, mint-green, hand-stitched silk shirt, nails done, mustache shaped, money in pocket, looking cleaner than the Board of Health.

He strolled into the poolroom slowly, arrogantly, paused in front of the cue rack and lit a cigarette, waiting for one of the ever-challenging suckers to give him a play.

Looking over the field, he nodded soberly to the dudes he knew and stared past the ones he didn't know.

One of the proven brotherhood, Sidney Robeson, better known as "Sidepockets," eased up to Elijah's left shoulder. "What's the word, bruh Sides?"

Sidepockets rolled the plastic martini toothpick around, from one side of his mouth to the other, before answering. "You got it, blood. I'm waitin' for mine to come in."

The two men zeroed in on a couple raw street boys at a far table, stroking superior sticks but talking too much shit.

After watching both of them make strategic errors in their game, Elijah and Sidepockets rechanneled their attentions to other tables, other possible challengers.

"Ohh, I . . . uh . . . just left Benny at the Tiger. Cat was really poppin', must've got into somethin' nice."

Elijah instantly reviewed all of the events of their recent venture together.

Yeahhh, he would do some shit like that. At some point during the night, while I was feelin' on Mabel's ass, he went down and cleaned up, got all the dough and stashed the pieces somewhere else. Sneaky, rat-faced son of a bitch! yeahhhh, he would do something like that.

He stared into Sidney's stone face and received all the reaffirmation he needed. Like, hey brother . . . and I know about the li'l piece of business you all took off on the other night.

Elijah nodded to Sidepockets and, trying to maintain his cool, strolled out of the Stickhall, jaws tighter than a bear trap, heading for the Tiger.

Fifty steps from the Stickhall, he escalated his stroll to a quick walk. Why? why? why? Why was it always necessary to bite chunks out of a dude's ass before you could get fair treatment, or a real understanding?

The closer he came to the Tiger Lounge, the madder he got. Li'l ol' chickenshit holdup man trying to beat me out of my righteously earned dough. Son of a bitch!

If a shadow of doubt remained, it was completely erased by the sight of Benny sitting at the bar between two psuedo-foxy ladies, stylin'.

Elijah eased up behind him and whispered. "Benny, lemme talk to you a minute?"

Benny turned, a trace of fright in his expression, a give-away to Elijah, and recovered. "Oh! hey, mannn, c'mon have a drink with me 'n my lady friends."

Elijah looked off to the other end of the bar, trying to

hold an even expression, not reveal the grim feelings he felt. "Later, brother," he replied with fake congeniality, "this won't take but a minute. I got somethin' heavy to lay on you."

Benny's eyes widened slightly, his greed being given something to feed on. "Somethin' heavy, huh?"

Elijah winked, pulling him in. "Yeahhh, somethin' really heavy. I know you'll go for it."

Benny signalled to Sly Bob, the bartender. "Keep the ladies happy, Bob . . . I be right back y'all."

Elijah walked out ahead of Benny, steaming.

Out front, he looked up and down the street, felt down in his pocket for his knife. Where could he go?

"Yeah, what's happenin'?" Benny asked urgently, anxious to be back with his party.

Elijah walked quickly to an apartment hallway a few doorways away, beckoning for Benny to follow. Benny frowned, but, being this much committed, he followed.

Elijah closed the hall door, pulled his blade out and snatched Benny across the hall by the collar. "Jiveass motherfucker! Did you have the nerve to try and hold out on me!?"

Benny, instantly aware of circumstances, went into his weasel act. "Hold on a minute, 'lijah . . . lemme explain . . . lemme . . ."

The veins in Elijah's temples puffed out. "Nigger! Do you know you coulda got me killed?! for nothin'!"

Benny tried to curl down into a knot. "Wait a minute, brother! I can explain! please!"

Elijah backhanded him across the face and began to

whack out at him with his knife, turning Benny's flailing hands and arms to bloody slashes.

After a dozen frenzied slashes with his knife, Elijah bent over Benny, sobbing and bleeding on the steps. "I oughta kill you. You know that, don't you? a lotta dudes would, tryin' to pull some rank shit like that on me!"

Benny held and squeezed his arms to his chest, deathly scared by the sight of the blood gushing out of him.

"Please, man! please! I'm dyin'! don't let me bleed to death, brother! please help me 'Lijah!"

"Pull out your pockets and gimme everything you got."

Benny dug down into his pockets, crying and getting blood on the roll of bills he pulled out.

Elijah kicked him in the nuts and slowly, methodically leafed through the roll. Twenty-five hundred dollars.

"This all of it?" he asked as Benny curled up on the floor of the hall, alternately holding his groin and squeezing the slashes on his arms to try to stop his bleeding.

"Benny, I asked you, is this all of it?"

"Yeahh! yeahh! that's all of it!" Benny almost screamed. "Help me get a doctor! I'm dyin', man! I'm dyin'!"

Elijah wiped the roll of bills and his knife blade off on Benny's hair.

"Die, motherfucker!" he said to him coldly and strolled out of the hall feeling righteous, as though he had corrected an injustice. He felt tempted to pop back into the Tiger, to tell the two women waiting for the rest of Benny's bankroll that he wouldn't be back, but decided to go on back to the Stickhall instead.

Sidepockets still stood near the cue rack, shifting his

weight from foot to foot occasionally.

"How 'bout it, my mannnnn?" he called out to Elijah above the clatter of the balls being racked, "shoot one for a fin?"

Elijah smiled and nodded. "Yeah, why not?"

Sidepockets pulled his favorite cue from the rack and thumped on the floor for the rack man.

They flipped coins for first shot, a small knot of hip players gathering coolly to watch two of the Stickhall's best get down. Elijah broke the triangle and stood off to one side as he watched Sidepockets methodically run the table.

"You got some blood on your 'shine, blood," Sidepockets mumbled out of the corner of his mouth as he took Elijah's money and thumped his stick for the rack man to rack 'em up again.

Elijah glanced at the toe of his shoe and frowned. Just like Benny, he'd even mess you up gettin' his ass kicked.

Elijah watched the young brother's approach. Twenty-two twenty-four years old. Half-ass slick . . . might go for it.

He stepped out of the doorway into a small flow of downtown shoppers, revved up to sell.

"Hey, looka here, young blood! I got somethin' twice as nice as a mother's advice."

He quickly matched the young brother's step and flashed, at thigh level, a velvet ring box with two glittering zircons in it. "Gimme twenty bones for both of 'em and take 'em on home!"

Elijah's sudden appearance, the glitter of the cheap rings,

the whole effect of things threw the young brother for a momentary loss.

He slackened his stride. "Uhh, I could really dig 'em, brother . . . but right now my coins is short."

Elijah pressed in, flashed the stones again, quickly, in the late afternoon sunlight. "I know you got *somethin'*, li'l bruh. Here, take a goooood look at these."

He flashed the glitter closer to the brother's face. In one split second, Elijah knew he had lost the sale. You could never tell. One person who would never think of buying anything in the streets might have a wild moment and buy everything. And on the other hand, some dude who bought anything and everything, habitually . . . might shy away from buying anything. You could never tell.

"Naw, man . . . sorry, I can't make it," the young brother finally decided and picked up his pace.

"Awright, blood . . . you had yo' chance," he called after him. And, like a cat licking himself after an insulting encounter, strolled over to a store front to check his image out, straighten the collar tips of his shirt, cock his brim at a more rakish angle.

He saw their reflections sweeping past him. Too good to be true.

"Pssssssstt! com'ere a minute, both o' y'all!"

Both of the soldiers turned his way in step.

"Huh? who? me?" the tallest of the two asked.

"Yeahhh! you, man. You! Both of y'all, come over here a minute," he half asked, half demanded.

As they approached him, he carefully checked them out. Twenty-year-olds. Clean-cut, hayseed types, whistling through on leave, muscle builders. He smiled pleasantly as they practically stood at attention in front of him.

"Yeah, what can we do for you, mister?"

Slight trace of some kind of other accent. Not Southern . . . he could place that in a second. Maybe semi-New England.

"Y'all can't do nothin' for me, but I can do two or three things for you."

He made a deliberate point of noticing the insignia on their sleeves. "Heyyy, are you guys in the same outfit my brother is in? Willie Roberts, First Brigade, Second Platoon?"

The two young soldiers, serious about everything, thought about it for a couple seconds. Finally, the shorter one, speaking for the two of them, announced hesitantly, "Nope, I don't b'lieve so. There's five, ten Negro . . . black guys in my unit and none of 'em is named Willie that I can recollect."

"Pretty rough, huh?" Elijah asked, pointing to the uniforms and all that it meant.

"We get by," the taller one said, an impatient tone in his voice. "Uhh, what was it you wanted, buddy? We're in a li'l bit of a hurry."

"Well," he started into his pitch coolly, softly. "When I said I could do two or three things for you, I really meant it."

He dug down into the pocket of his super-lightweight sports coat and pulled out a ring box. He checked the secret mark on it carefully, to make certain that he didn't have the wrong box . . . and opened it with the tasteful movements of a first-class jeweler. "The first is this," he swept the ring past their eyes in a tight arch.

"You guys from outta town?" he asked, posing a superficial question to ease their feelings along.

"Yeah, how'd you guess?" the tall one asked sarcastically.

"Ohh, just thinkin', just thinkin'. I figure you'd be able to get good money for this outta town. Anywhere outta town. My brother sent it to me, got it off some gook in Laos or Thailand or one o' those places . . . sent it to me and I can't even pawn it. Gimme fifty dollars for it and it's all yours. Either one of you." He allowed the late sun to strike the heart of the red glass again.

The taller one exchanged a sly glance with his friend. "How much is it worth?"

Elijah pinned him closely, the eternal mark trying to be nickel slick. "Ooooooohhh . . . three hundred, at least. I'd keep it if I wasn't down on my luck. I bet your girl back home would really trip out on somethin' like this."

He paused and did a quick study of how their eyes lit up, just enough to let him know that he had struck a chord. "Sayyyy, talkin' 'bout girls, not that I'm tryin' to take you away from your *true* loves or nothin' like that, but I know a broad . . ." He stopped his rapid-fire monologue to trace a Coca Cola bottle shape in mid-air. He knew he had them, in one fashion or another. Sometimes it was hard to tell which hook, which angle the sucker would hang himself on. For white men, black women were a very powerful hook, especially being recommended by a black dude. "And if that ain't enough," he continued, "she's got a friend."

The short soldier looked closely at Elijah and started to ask, "Uhhh . . . is she . . . uhh?"

"Both black as lumps o' coal!" he stated emphatically, "but let's deal with that after we get this other thang out of the way."

The three men edged over to the inside of the sidewalk to allow the five o'clock types free passage.

"How much did you say?"

"Fifty bucks!" Elijah shot back at him.

"Fifty dollars?! Heyyyy, that's kinda steep for my pocket," the short one announced and looked up to his tall buddy.

Elijah, feeling the hook slip, quickly rebaited it. "Hell! who am I to quibble 'round with a couple groovy young soldiers. Gimme forty-five and I'll buy us a beer to clinch the deal, whaddaya say?"

The two soldiers exchanged shrugs and well-we-don't-know-about-that-shit looks.

"Tell ya what," the tall started off, ruminating on his effort to be slick. "Why don't we . . . why don't we knock off five more bucks and skip the beer?"

Elijah looked off into the gutter for a few seconds, a pained expression on his face. "Mannnnnn, you must've been a fuckin' horse trader before you and Uncle Sam got hooked up."

"Nope, never traded any, but I busted my share of 'em, up in Stray Bear, Montana." The tall soldier subconsciously puffed his chest out.

Elijah winked at the short guy, a fake, jive, hip, conspiratorial wink, and conceded, "Awwwright, shit! gimme forty lousy ass dollars! damn! What in the world are you young dudes learnin' these days?!"

The two men, partners in many minor league transactions in the past, pulled out twenty dollars apiece and handed it to him.

He opened the ring box to take one more look at his "reluctantly" sold gem. "You dudes don't have to bullshit me, I know the first thing you gon' do, when you get back to camp, is re-sell this stone for a hundred, at least . . . you knew how much it was worth when I opened the box up."

The three of them openly exchanged smiles all around for the first time.

Elijah glanced from one smiling young, weatherbeaten face to the other. Surprising, he thought, how easy it is to rip a chump off and then boost his ego sky-high by making him believe that he had done the ripping.

He looked down at the ring box and had a wild urge to let them take one last look and then palm it. But, what the hell! why add insult to injury?

He dropped the box into the short soldier's hand. Both of them stared at the ring box and then into his face, seemingly reluctant to dissolve such an exotic relationship.

Elijah started easing off into the afternoon traffic, his streetologist's sense of theatre telling him, now is the time for the exit.

"Uhhh, hey buddy!" the tall one called and beckoned with a crooked finger at him.

For a split second Elijah was tempted to run. Could these dudes be the police? Nawwwww, intuition told him they just couldn't be. "Yeah, what now? y'all got my life's blood now, what else do you want?" he funned at them, hoping he wouldn't sound too cold. He placed himself at an oblique angle, ready to hat up, just in case.

The tall one leaned into his ear. "Would you happen to

know where we could get some good smoke?"

Elijah cocked his head to one side, as though he hadn't heard right. "Huhh?"

"I said," the soldier repeated, "would you happen to know where we could cop some good smoke?"

Elijah pursed his lips and looked at the two of them seriously. "Yeahhhh, yeah, I know where you can cop . . . really good shit too, straight outta Cambodia."

The short one, unable to contain the enthusiasm, exclaimed, "Yeahhh! really!?"

Elijah nodded, amazed, once again, at how easy it was to form a relationship with his "clients."

"Right on . . . all you have to do is follow me. Don't follow too closely though. I'm sure you all know, by now, that I'm a 'businessman,' and you know how closely some people watch 'businessmen.'" He made a neat about-face, and started off, not really knowing where he would lead them, but certain that it would be in the right direction.

They followed, the prey behind the animal that was feeding on them. He led them off the side street, away from relative cool, onto the heat of the main stem.

After a couple blocks, he stopped in front of one of the city's largest, most efficient-looking office buildings and turned to the two soldiers. They eased up to him in the middle of the bustling, mid-evening, on-their-way-to-home crowds, trying to look hip.

"Here?! this the place?" the tall soldier asked suavely . . . trying to be hip.

Elijah nestled in on them, playtime over. "Uh huhhhn," he murmured, barely glancing at the building, and the people streaming out of it. "This is it, *the* place. There's a lawyer sellin' the best shit in town, on the thirteenth floor."

"Wowwww!" The tall one finally relented, releasing his pent-up enthusiasm. A ruby ring from a black dude for forty bucks *and* some Cambodian grass. How much more could you get away with in one day, especially with Tommy the Runt?

Elijah gauged his thought patterns and swept in, anxious, now, to get rid of them.

"Awright, how much you want?"

"How much is it?" the short asked.

"How much do you want?" Elijah squeezed out of the side of his mouth. "I can get you a motherfuckin' pound, if that's what you want."

The two soldiers stood, looking stunned for a moment, the last thought in their heads. "A pound!?"

"Well?" he dug at them fiercely, making them feel like pootbutts. "How much? I got things to do, I can't stand here all night."

"Uhh, how 'bout . . . uhhh, twenty bucks' worth?" the tall one shot in.

"Cool!" Elijah shot back at him. "Gimme twenty-five, that's two dimes 'n a nickel, in 'business' language. I get five dollars as commission for doin' the good deed."

The two soldiers, suddenly realizing that they were just small-time American boys, from places where people left their front doors unlocked, blinked in unison. And then divided the price of the grass between them, and the "commission." Twelve dollars and fifty cents apiece.

Elijah smiled indulgently and looked off into the distance

as they surreptitiously placed the money in his hand.

"It's really good, huh?" the short one asked.

"Dynamite!" Elijah replied emphatically, and marched into the office building lobby.

"Wait for me in the lobby," he said over his shoulder. He let the two men see him wink at the elevator starter as though he were in cahoots and caught the elevator upward.

On the third floor he skipped off the elevator, looking around for the rear exit. He wandered around the third floor, peeking into the offices, checking out the unguarded typewriters and the other office paraphernalia, feeling frustrated after ten minutes, not being able to find the rear exit.

The middle-aged black man pushing the scrub bucket down the long office building hallway saved him. "Hey, looka here, brother," Elijah probed at him casually, certain of the cohesion between them. "Where's the rear exit stairs? I'm parked out back."

The gray-haired black man looked up at him, four hundred years of tricks and antics in his grained brown eyes, and jerked his head toward a door Elijah had missed.

"Gon' through there, it'll let you out down in the alley."

"Sho' wanta thank ya, brotherman," Elijah mumbled at him, striding toward the door.

He breathed a complete sigh of relief on the way out . . . sixty-five dollars to the ghetto's good.

CHAPTER 5

Elijah sat in a back booth of the Tiger Lounge with a sometime hustling buddy nicknamed Big Toe, listening to the house combo play a funky blues and to a would-be scheme of Big Toe's.

"Man, I'm tellin' you, it's a lead-pipe cinch!"

Elijah took a long sip from his drink, already fifteen good-time, finger-poppin' dollars into his afternoon rip-off.

"The last nigger who shot me into that 'lead-pipe cinch' shit damned near got his throat cut."

Big Toe turned his glass around in the water ring it had made on the table.

"Yeahhh, yeah," Toe replied impatiently, "I heard about the shit that went down between you and Benny . . . but, hey, looka here, man . . . you know Benny always has been a treacherous motherfucker! The thang I'm runnin' down to you is strictly on the up 'n up."

Both men felt the atmosphere of the club tighten up, the casual conversations cease, and knew why instinctively.

The two detectives, Murphy and Jackson, strolled to the back booth, stood over Elijah and Big Joe, weighted down by shoulder holsters and authority.

"Uhh, good evenin', Officer Murphy . . . uhhh, Officer Jackson," Toe mumbled nervously.

"Don't speak to us, thief . . . 'til we speak to you, dig it?" Murphy growled and glared at him.

"You the boss, Officer Murphy sir, you the boss," Toe answered cautiously, not wanting to run any risks.

"Let's take a walk, Elijah," Jackson said to Elijah. Elijah, trying to front it off, sipped at his drink before replying. "Take a walk, where?"

Murphy, two hundred and fifteen pounds behind the whiskey on his breath, leaned across the table into Elijah's face. "Don't sit back on your ass tryin' to be cute with me, I said, let's take a walk, now move goddamn it!"

Elijah almost spilled his drink complying with the command. It didn't pay to take things too far with Murphy and Jackson because they believed in police brutality as a matter of course, and everyone who knew them knew that.

Elijah hurriedly arranged himself between the two of them and walked out of the lounge, trying to maintain his cool and be meek at the same time.

They walked him to their unmarked car under the side-view looks of the street corner regulars, out for the night's doin's, late working people and an assorted collection of just plain ol' 47th Street folks.

Jackson drove them to the forty-five hundred block of St. Lawrence Avenue and parked. Elijah breathed a little easier . . . at least this was no bust. Probably a shakedown. Or maybe they wanted him to stool.

He pulled his cigarettes out of his shirt pocket, lit up and slumped back beside Murphy.

"What's happenin', Murph? You acted like you was gon' chew my nuts off back there in the joint."

Murphy smiled across the distance between them maliciously. "I've told you two or three times, brotherman. Stop tryin' to be cute with me. I started to knock you on your ass."

Jackson smiled up into the rear-view mirror at the exchange, carefully placed his .357 mag on the front seat and pulled a half-pint of good whiskey out of the glove compartment.

He took a long pull and passed it to Murphy. Murphy almost drained it and passed the corner to Elijah.

Elijah turned the bottle up, a little high already, but trying to be cool, steady about the whole business. What the fuck was going down?

"Uggggh!" he shuddered, giving a little show for his captors. "I'd rather smoke dope any day than drink that rotgut."

"You may not be able to get either one for a bit, from the way things look," Murphy dug in at him, his malicious sense of humor on display again.

"Heyyyy, what's the deal?" Elijah probed at him with a soft, nervous smile.

"Homer, you break it down to 'im, you done had the most trainin' in law."

Jackson, Murphy's natural bone partner, draped his right arm across the back of the seat and began, pedantically. "Wellll, brother . . . here it is, in a nutshell. Looks like you and Benny held up the wrong crap game the other night."

Elijah, as scheduled, exclaimed, "Crap game!? What crap game?"

"Awwww c'mon off it, man!" Murphy dug him hard in the ribs. "Save that bullshit for the other police."

"Evidently," Jackson continued, "evidently you 'n Benny didn't check into things too closely, else you never would've stuck up li'l John Diamond's joint."

Elijah looked out at the smoked-up buildings around him, the dark figures passing the car, feeling sick at the pit of his stomach. "Li'l John Diamond? Is he a big dude with a pinkie ring on his left hand?"

"That's right!" Murphy laughed at the expression on Elijah's face, cupping the bulk at his own wasteline with both hands. "Hahhh hahhh hahhaha, yeahhhh, that's right, a big fat dude with a li'l diamond ring on his do-do finger."

"Anyway," Jackson moved along, "to make a long story short, Li'l John, knowin' the right people, put three grand on the wire for you and Benny, which Murph and me are goin' to split right down the middle for bringin' you and Benny in."

Murphy closed Elijah's beginning protest off with a wave of his hand. "We pulled Benny in this afternoon, stitches everywhere but under the bottom of his feet. It's a wonder the poor fool ain't dead from loss o' blood."

Jackson winked in fake-warm fashion to Elijah. "Benny ain't got no blood, has he, brother?"

Elijah ignored Jackson's attempt at joking, took a deep breath and started into some heavy conning.

"Looka here, Murph, both of you dudes are righteous brothers. Lemme slide and I'll make it worth your while. I promise on my momma's grave, even if I have to send it back by carrier pigeon."

Murphy smirked. "Now, we thought you'd propose somethin' weird like that . . . Officer Jackson?"

Jackson cleared his throat, playing his role to the bus stop. "Well, you see . . . it's like this, Elijah. We couldn't let you slide, even if we wanted to . . . for three or four good reasons.

"Number one: you'd probably never be able to send us anything from anywhere, because you'd more 'n likely be dead. Li'l John offered the reward for you two dead or alive. You should be happy we got to you before they did."

"Number two: Benny sang like Ray Charles the minute we got his ass in the car."

"Guess he thought we was gon' pop some of his stitches loose," Murphy added with a tight smile.

"Number three: it'll look good for us, you know, bringin' in a dangerous suspect. I mean, like, we couldn't really let you slide after everybody had seen us pick you up, now could we?"

"What would people think, baby?" Murphy widened his smile into a cruel grin.

"And last, but not least," Jackson exhaled, "we are both po', broke, black and dee-terminated to up hold the law. Can you dig where we be comin' from?"

Murphy leaned forward to give his partner five. "Right

on, brother! right on!"

Elijah winced as though the slapping of their palms was a blow to his cheek.

"Whoa! hold up a minute! I know damned well Li'l John, or nobody else is gon' try to lay a case on me for . . . uhhh . . ."

"Allegedly," Jackson supplied the legal term.

He really is a chickenshit motherfucker, Elijah thought.

"Yeahhh, that's right! for allegedly holdin' up an *illegal* gamblin' joint."

Murphy shook his head with disgust. "Awwww, c'mon on now, blood . . . you ain't usin' your head. You know better than that, that wouldn't even come up in court."

"Awright then," Elijah pulled his trump out, "if it can't be that, what's the beef?"

Murphy, still playing cue card, signalled graciously to Jackson with a wave of his big right hand.

"Detective Jackson, would you be so kind?"

Jackson made a fist and popped a finger out to illustrate each point.

"Grand theft, auto. I guess you know Benny was drivin' a stolen vehicle, assault with a deadly weapon . . . that's right, on Benny, receivin' stolen goods, we been knowin' about that for a long time."

"Hey man, forget about what we might stick you with, we can think somethin' up on the way downtown. Li'l John wants your ass off the streets for a while and we want three grand."

Elijah's head slumped to his chest, wondering if he could slug Murphy with the bottle and try to make it.

Jackson, reading his mind, quietly pointed his piece over

the seat at Elijah's head.

"You better put the cuffs on him, I feel some bad vibes startin' to creep up."

Murphy backhanded him in the mouth.

"You wasn't thinkin' about doin' anything nasty, was you?"

Elijah glared at him. Motherfucker! and threw the empty whiskey bottle out of the open window and held his hands up for the cuffs. Popped again. It never failed . . . just as everything was beginning to get together.

"Behind, my man, you know how we do it," Murphy stated in a matter-of-fact voice.

Elijah held his hands behind him for the cold manacles, slumped back into the seat after they were shackled on. Well, at least I'll be able to get a good lawyer with the dough from the holdup. Wonder what those people out at the airport will think when they open up that locker and pull out that suitcase with bricks in it?

"What's funny, brotherman?" Murphy asked, his fist raised for another mouth shot.

"Ooohhh, nothin', really . . . I was just wonderin' if me 'n Benny would wind up in the same cell."

"We'll try to see what we can arrange." Jackson smiled pleasantly at him in the rear-view mirror. "Yeahhh, we'll try to see what we can arrange."

The weeks in the county jail, the filth of it, the sight and sound of the homosexual assaults on the younger, more innocent prisoners, the clanging of steel doors, the involved legal language, the torture of not really knowing what was going to happen flashed through Elijah's mind as he stood in front of the crusty-headed old white man in his black robes.

He had resisted Leelah's pleas to get a "good Jewish lawyer," somebody that Browney the Fence had recommended, decided instead to have a brother defend him.

" 'Ey mon," Nick the Geech had warned him during a visit, "you'd best be dahmed careful ya don't get forty years with the brother defendin'."

Elijah had laughed at him and kept the faith. Now he was at the moment of truth, the point where all the legal hassling gave way to the decision that the judge would make.

"I hereby sentence you to a term of one year and one day in the county jail," came to him as though someone were speaking through a foghorn.

"Bailiff, remove the prisoner, next case!"

A year and a day. A year and a day. A year and a day . . . Elijah muttered in his mind being led away, smiling sickly at Leelah crying, Nick the Geech, Big Toe, Zelma, Precious Percy and three other fringe members of their circle who had decided to brave the daytime in order to see him sentenced.

His lawyer gave him a soul shake and a pain-filled look. "Sorry, blood . . . I did the best I could."

"I ain't got no complaints, man," Elijah spoke between clenched teeth, on the verge of tears . . . not because of the year and a day itself, but because he was going to have to do it in the lousy ass county jail.

He sat over in a corner of the bullpen casually studying

the weirdos, the diamond-hard cliques, the homo triangles, the chess game that seemed to have started from the day he was brought in, nine months earlier.

Nine months. Elijah slumped down on the wooden bench, feeling gritty under the arms from not washing, a strong crotch funk floating up to his nostrils.

Nine months in the county jail. He turned his attention back to his fellow inmates, avoiding the seductive looks of a couple drag queens . . . nine months in the county jail, dead time, nothing to do but scrounge, scheme, connive and sit up in the bullpen listening, looking, thinking.

"Hey man, you got a cigarette?"

Elijah looked up into the face of the figure in front of him and almost answered, automatically, no, buy your own, motherfucker. But, in a moment of compassion—like, after all, the dude was just a simple alimony hostage who didn't know his ass from a hole in the ground—he flicked him a cigarette from his pack . . . what the hell. The man took the cigarette, nodding gratefully, lit up and stood near Elijah puffing deeply.

"Wowwww, sho' feels good to smoke, 'specially when you ain't done it in a li'l while."

Elijah frowned at the late middle-aged black man, turning him off. He had enough to think about, the last thing he needed was the clammy friendship of a dumb sap doing bad time on an alimony beef. The man made a few more hesitant attempts at conversation and then wandered away after receiving no encouragement.

Elijah looked at his back, a dozen descriptions of what he thought of the man swelling up in his head. Mark. Chump.

Sucker. Sap. Asshole. Fool. In jail for non-payment of alimony. Shit! the chump had probably been supporting some jiveass bitch for days, missed two payments and she had gotten him locked up, incarcerated, as they said in the joint.

He stared at the man's back as he took his place on the fringe of a circle of dudes arguing, jawing at each other, as usual. What else was there to do in the county jail, after the watery oatmeal, crusty toast and slimy coffee?

"All I'm sayin' to you, stupid ass, ignunt motherfucker, is that, in order to believe the truth, you have to first hear it, and I'll bet you two cartons of cigarettes against your grimy asshole that you wouldn't recognize the truth if you heard it, simply because you've never been told anything but lies, all your black ass life!"

Elijah slumped a little lower on the bench, tired of the sounds of the eternal discussions, debates, that started from the time they were clanged awake 'til the time they were told, "Lights out, beddy bye!"

"I know what the truth is, chump," a bass voice thumped back at the other voice. "The truth is . . . listen to me! goddamn it! don't be standin' there playin' with your nuts and lookin' all smug!"

"I am listenin' to you. I can play with my nuts if I want to, they mine!"

The group of men in the circle around the two men laughed, subconsciously thankful that anyone could provide them with some kind of outlet.

The two debaters, recognizing jailhouse debating etiquette, paused to allow the cynical laughter to die down.

"Awright, here is the truth. Damned near every one of

us in here is a hostage of the state."

"A what? What's that you say, brother?" a voice deep in the circle called out for clarification.

"I said that damned near every one of us in here is a hostage of the state. The reason why, mainly, is because we, us black folks, have never realized, not since they lied to us and told us we were free, that we were being conditioned to be slaves in another kind of way."

Elijah glanced across the large enclosure at a small, tightly knit group of motorcycle club members, the Nazi Brother Group, someone had nicknamed them. The group turned red in the face collectively as they attempted to ignore the black speakers.

Elijah decided to join the circle around the speakers.

He slouched with a cigarette in his jibbs, a cynical attitude showing for all to see. The same old bullshit. Every monk in the cell had been a major league player out in the world, every holdup man had been a bank robber, all of them were innocent.

The talk was so often lost in the stars, abstractions poured out by semi-literate mack men.

"The only difference between you and him, between you and the upper echelon rip-off artist, who is the white boy, don't make no doubt about that! you unnerstand! The only difference between you and them is that they've convinced and conditioned your black ass to a certain level!

"Dig it!" The speaker, a bull-voiced toad of a black man, with biceps running all up behind his neck, flung his arms out to have his statements embrace the whole group. "Do you realize how devastatin' the white boy's game has been

By Odie Hawkins

on your ass!? huh!? do you!? Are you aware, brother?! are
you aware that we got geniuses standin' 'round here, right
now! motherfuckers who be standin' out on corners dealin'
with mo' complications, mo' bullshit and I don't know
what all, than the average college boy ever dreamed of?"

The man speaking opposite him attempted to pop back
in, on an ego trip more than anything else.

Elijah felt surprised to hear his voice joined to those who
shouted the ego tripper down. "Be cool, man! Let brother
speak on! brother speaks well!"

The bull voice looked around the group with a cold glint
in his eye, hard to tell whether he was trying to dish out
sincere info, or play the new game.

"When I say that we all are hostages of the state, what I
mean is that because they've never had any categories for
the various sections of streetologists, which takes in most of
us, we wind up doin' shit that is declared illegal, but actually
is shit that they be doin' legally, and gettin' away with it!
Now what I'm sayin' to you, about truth, is this! As an ele-
ment of nature and consequently, one of being, is this!"

Elijah wandered away from the group, back over to his
corner, a slightly irritated frown on his brow.

It never failed. No matter how much sense some of the
jailhouse debaters seemed to be making when they started
off; somehow, to his mind, they always seemed to veer off
somewhere.

The brother did have a point, though, he admitted to
himself as he slumped back down into his spot. Yeahhh, the
brother did have a point . . . they *were* hostages. He had
two points. They were also conditioned like hell to stay

where they had been programmed to be. He smiled, in spite of the sadness he felt settle over him. "Conditioned to be slaves in another kind of way."

Yeahhh, they were slaves all right. New World slaves in another time, another dimension, playing the same old games.

The sounds from the men across from him became noises. He nodded to himself, as though agreeing to something someone had said. That was the other thing about the whole business.

No matter how logically they started off, it always seemed to degenerate into some kind of formless merry-go-round, something like a group of pick-up conga drummers in the park who refused to play together because they feared success.

No wonder niggers have such a helluva hard time gettin' it together . . . we all afraid that we'll lose our whatever it is we got to lose if we get together.

Elijah looked at one of the drag queens filing his nails and thought about his woman Leelah, and Dee Dee, and Mabel Stewart. He crossed his legs, trying to push his hardening jones down between his thighs, to keep his thang cooled out, like, after all, three more months was a pretty good piece of time to remain unfucked. Three more fuckin' months! He found himself wishing that they had laid a case on him strong enough to stick him into the penitentiary anyway.

The penitentiary was clean, the guards were long-winded civil servants doing time along with the cons, looking forward to a vacation every year and a pension at the end of thirty-five years on the job.

"Could I get another one of your cigarettes, brother?" the alimony man asked politely, trembling from his nicotine addiction.

"Buy your own cigarettes, motherfucker!" Elijah bristled up at him, wanting, for some reason, to kick the square in the ass.

The man backed off, startled to find the generous type that he had conned out of a cigarette a short time ago so mean and evil.

Elijah uncrossed his legs and enjoyed the feeling of having his dick swell up along the side of his thighs.

Three more fuckin' months. Ninety more days. He uncoiled himself to wander over to the drinking fountain, and back to the edge of the circle, two more speakers scuffling with each other's logic, or lack of it.

Oh well, what the hell . . . who knows? somebody might lay something on me that I can use when they cut me loose.

Wonder what Leelah's doing? Haven't heard from her in three weeks now.

An endless parade of bowls of watery oatmeal, dried-out toast and slimy coffee-days slid back and forth in front of Elijah's eyes.

Why in the fuck don't they come on and cut me loose? As he restlessly wandered around the bullpen, it seemed that his fellow inmates were constantly bumping into him, getting in his way, causing him to be pissed off about one thing or another.

"Baker! Barker! Brookes! Burns!" the guard bellowed

out to a suddenly silent group of men.

Elijah tossed his cigarette pack over into the alimony man's lap and gathered his shoebox bull of belongings together.

"Thanks, man," the alimony man called out to him, hating him for being freed.

"Brookes, Elijah?"

"Righteously!"

"Don't be funny, asshole," the guard spoke in a monotone, checking names off on his clipboard.

Elijah kept a straight face, his armpits suddenly damp from nervous perspiration. Anything! Anything! anything at all, Mr. Guard! just please let me out of this terrible fucked-up hole! Let me out of this open shithouse with all the do-do running down the dank, gray, institutional walls, filled with the scratchings 'n scribblings of a thousand penned-up minds. Let me out, please, let me out, please . . .

"Okay, you dudes are being processed for release, follow me."

The four men followed the guard and his precious clipboard through one clanging, barred gate after another.

Funny, Elijah thought, as they came into the administration section, all clean and sterile. Funny that the only dudes getting out with me are last-named B. Ohh well, what the hell! I'm getting out! damn coincidences.

Look out streets! here I come!

CHAPTER 6

Elijah braced himself up on his knuckles and stared down into the woman's face.

What difference did it make that it wasn't Leelah, or Dee Dee? What difference did it make? pussy was pussy.

He studied the contorted expression on her face. Was she in pain, or did it feel good?

He smiled . . . had it been that long? so long that he couldn't tell whether or not he was causing a woman pain or pleasure?

He frowned, studying her expression more closely under the dim blue bulb . . . yes, it was pleasure. What bitch wouldn't feel pleasure snatching a nigger's nuts out of the sand that had been dragging as long as his had.

She looks a li'l bit like Mabel. Wowwww! the thought jarred his movement to a sudden stop. Mabel . . .

For the first time since they'd picked each other up in the Swan Song, she asked him a question. "What's the matter, baby?"

"Nothin', ain't nothin' wrong" . . . he answered her lamely, revving himself back up to a slow jelly, trying to come again.

Nawwww, ain't nothing wrong, Momma . . . nothing at all. I just got out of the slams, my true blue lady didn't come for me, and ain't where we used to be, my gritty-nitty girlfriend is shacked up with a jealous card player, one half of my so-called friends don't know me and the other half don't want to know me . . . like, what good is a player with no play?

He jacked the tempo of his movement up and gently curled the woman's thighs up over his hips . . . she responded to his movement with a belly dancer's thrust of her pelvis.

Wowwww! this bitch really knows how to fuck!

"Uhhh, what's your name?"

The woman went slack for a moment and then tightened up all over him laughing.

Her laughter was so contagious that he found himself caught up in it, each muscular contraction of her stomach forcing him closer to a climax.

"Hahhhhahhh . . . uhhh . . . what's so funny?" he asked, trying to slide back into the mellow groove they had.

"You are," she answered in a heavy, whiskey-scarred voice.

"Oh yeahhh, why is that?" he probed, sustaining his moves and praying that he hadn't grabbed a neurotic off the bar stool.

110

"Men never seem to be satisfied 'til they find out the lady's name, they even ask whores, what's your name?"

He responded to her observation with a slow nod and stopped his dance.

"You're right! you know that?"

"I know I am," she answered, and looked at him with a challenge in her eyes.

The dim blue light, the grime of the drab hotel furniture arranged around the bed quietly faded out of his consciousness as he felt her vagina grip his penis and milk the sap from it.

After a few seconds, the intensity of it taking him on a quick, magic ride, he kissed her mouth very gently and whispered into her ear.

"I love you, woman . . . whatever your name is."

She squeezed his face into her breasts and mumbled, "You guessed it, that's exactly what my name is, Woman."

He rolled slowly off of her body, spent . . . and stretched out to stare up at the bulb.

What's next? After a woman, it would be nice to have some girl, but first, in order to do that he would have to get in touch with Browney the Fence.

The woman curled up into the crook of his shoulder.

"Tell me what your name is, you didn't, you know?"

"My name is Man, baby . . . my name is Man," he said softly and faded off into a deep sexual catnap.

Elijah found himself breathing a little harder with excitement as he stepped into the telephone booth to call Browney. Automatically he dialed into their code . . . three rings,

111

hang up . . . two rings, hang up, and then let it ring.

If there was anybody who would help him get his shit back together again, it would be old cold-blooded ass Browney. Hmmf! for all the good it did me, I may as well have had a public defender and not blew all that dough . . . at least I would've had something left for a stake when I got back out here.

"Yeah!" the gruff voice suddenly replaced the dial tone. Same old Browney . . .

"What's to it, Browney? This is Elijah."

"Eli . . . Elijah, well, I'll be! is it really you? I figured you for next month."

Elijah curled his lips down with a frown. Chickenshit motherfucker, probably got a calendar with every nigger's jail term marked off that he be dealing with.

"You can X me for this month. I'm back on the scene. Can you do me any good?"

Elijah's mind flickered to the patented picture of Browney, leaning back in his stuffed leather chair, waving his secretary out of the room, telling her to accept no more calls from anyone for the next three minutes.

Browney the Fence, used cars, a piece of a record company, a vehement supporter of capitalism in every form, a wheeler dealer.

"Whatcha got, buddy-o?" Browney asked cautiously.

"I ain't got a goddamned thing, man . . . that's why I'm callin' you."

Browney's caution skipped from there to outright coldness, now that the reading had been made.

"Uhh, what can I do for you?"

112

Elijah, mistaking the chill for someone requesting a price list, shot back, "I need a whole gang o' thangs . . . but they all add up to one thing. Money, honey. I need some clothes and a decent ride." .

Browney shifted his bulk around in his chair and swung his heels up onto his desk, searching in his desk drawer for a pack of cigarettes.

"Damn it!"

"Huh?!"

"Awwww hahh hah, I wasn't talkin' to you, buddy-o, I just discovered I was out of cigarettes. 'Scuse me a sec. Uhhh, Norene! come in here a minute, willya doll?"

Browney's secretary, a Chicana and an ex-wise lady of the barrio, stood in the doorway with an inscrutable expression on her face. The fat greasy bastard!

"How 'bout runnin' out for a pack o' cigarettes, doll? Take it out of petty cash. How much do you figure, buddy-o?" He slid from the lady in the door back to Elijah without a pause.

"I could really get down on two grand or thereabouts, yeahhh, two grand would do it. I still owe my lawyer a few . . ."

"Two grand? that's a lotta dough, buddy-o?"

"How much do you want on it?" Elijah snapped. "I need it for a month, maybe less."

"Awww Elijah, EEElijahhh," Browney responded with a large dose of contrived sympathy in his voice, "you wouldn't hafta gimme anything on it, nothin'! if I had it you could get it, like that!"

The telephone booth suddenly seemed much smaller.

"Sounds like you tryin' to tell me somethin'."

Browney paused for a few seconds to allow what he had said to Elijah to sink in.

"Well, two grand is a lotta dough, Elijah."

"Awww c'mon on, man! don't gimme that shit! When I was out in the streets I was layin' at least two grand worth o' stuff on you every week, and what was I gettin' for it? peanuts! and now you gon' try to tell me you can't stake me for . . . ?"

"Now just a minute!" Browney interrupted abruptly, "hold on there a minute! then was then and now is now. Deals made yesterday are old deals. What we wanna talk about are new deals, right? right! Tell ya what, gimme a ring tomorrow afternoon. Maybe I can hit you with a couple C-notes."

Elijah held the phone away from his ear as though he hadn't heard right.

"A couple bills, huh? Lissen to me close, you motherless white motherfucker! I tell you what you can do. You can stuff those measly two bills up your fat ass!"

He slammed the telephone back onto the hook and leaned back against the panes of the telephone booth, perspiration streaming down his face.

Two of the neighborhood winos slowly made their way past the booth, eyes bleary, looking for another short dog.

Elijah kicked his heel against the back of the booth with frustration. Who in the hell else could he call on? Damn!

The booth seemed to get tighter, to almost the suffocation point, as he slowly dialed Browney's code again.

"Yeah!" The same abrupt snarl, not caring whether it

was Elijah calling back or not, but knowing that it was. Or someone else, no matter.

"Heyyyy Browney, look, this is Elijah again." Elijah spoke in deliberately even tones. "Forget about what I just said. How much did you say you'd let me have?"

"Two bills, tops."

"Make it three, okay?" Elijah said, trying not to sound as though he were begging.

"Why not? we're ol' friends. Three bills it is."

"Cool. When can I get it?"

"That'll be a quarter on the dollar, buddy-o."

Elijah's lips parted for a moment to release some vile language, but reconsidered his position. "Yeahhh, yeah, okay, whatever you say."

"My man will get it to you tomorrow afternoon. You still hanging out at that Tiger joint?"

"I'll be there tomorrow afternoon," he spoke softly, resigned to dealing with the Dealer. "Thanks, thanks for everything," he signed off sarcastically.

"Don't mention it. Just make sure you don't miss any payments, I got a couple guys over here who don't do anything but leg work for me."

Elijah hung up the telephone coolly, cursing the voice, the man and everything he represented.

The thought buzzed through his skull as he left the humidity of the telephone booth, to hit the heat of the streets. "I got a couple guys over here who don't do anything but leg work for me." Best be careful with that bastard, I don't know what I'd do with both of my legs broke.

He stopped for a newspaper and strolled slowly down

51st Street, heading for Malcolm X Park and a thorough study of the want ads. One of the good pieces of advice given him by one of the slickest dudes in jail had been: "Get a job, man . . . work on it for a bit. You know they gon' be watchin' you for a while. Throw 'em off a li'l bit, confuse 'em, that way you can get away with a whole bunch o' shit." Yeah, a gig. Wowwww! it's been ten years since I hit a lick at a snake. Let's see what we got here . . .

Elijah carefully wove a sparkling figure-eight pattern onto the length of the long hallway, enjoying the rhythm of the buffer. He suavely flicked the swirling brush around at the end of the hallway, paused to look out at the downtown lights surrounding him, and started back, repolishing the gleaming surface, his mind a little vacant from the monotony of his actions.

The lady at the County Concentrated Employment office had been diplomatic and helpful.

"Please, Mr. Brookes, don't feel for a second that the . . . uhhh . . . that your recent incarceration will act against you in any way. We have a large number of brothers coming through our agency who've just been released, or who have served time. We try to deal with the needs of the people and not whether or not they've been . . . uhhh . . . in jail or not."

He pressed the *off* button on the buffer at the opposite end of the hallway, gently laid the handle of the buffer down and dug into his shirt pocket for the last joint in his stash.

Walking quickly past the empty offices to make certain

that no one was working at eleven p.m., he stood at the half-opened window at the end of the hallway and lit up.

Downtown Chicago, the four-to-twelve shift. A custodian. City lights . . . his playground. He found himself unable to repress a smile as he sucked down to the roach.

A working man, an "employee," a member of the "proletariat," someone in the joint had once called it.

Thirty-one years old. The smile faded. Emptying waste baskets and buffing floors. In debt to Nasty Browney. Couldn't even borrow a dime from supposed to be "friends."

Thirty-one years old. In and out of institutions since sixteen or thereabouts. Supposed to be slick. Shit!

He flicked the fingernail stub of the joint out of the window and tried to follow its flight down through the canyon, to the street, sixteen stories below.

Loaded now, feeling mellow, he braced himself on his elbows and leaned the top of his body out of the window, trying to think/dream himself away from the two hallways left to be buffed.

The smell of Lake Michigan backed up in his nose for a few minutes, braced on a strong evening breeze. Chicago in the summertime. The summertime, the spring and the fall.

He shivered involuntarily, thinking about the coming winter. Winter was always coming, and there was nothing in the world you could do about it.

"Sorry to disturb you, Brookes."

Elijah bumped the back of his head pulling himself out of the window. The foreman of the building's custodians, a large, grim-faced black dude who always seemed to be prowling around, trying to catch someone doing something they shouldn't be doing, glared down into Elijah's face.

"Like I said, Mr. Brookes, sorry to disturb you, but shouldn't you be buffin' the floors?"

The throbbing pain in the back of his head, amplified by the smoke, made Elijah speechless for a few seconds, as he stood glaring back at Samuel S. Simon.

"Mannnnn," he finally managed to say, as the first flush of pain subsided. "Don't be sneakin' up on me like . . . like . . ."

"That's my job, Brookes! to be sneakin' up on people. We got a contract to fill, now how about doin' the rest of these floors?!"

Elijah stared at the man's broad, muscular back as he turned away abruptly and walked back down the hall, to sneak up on some other wrongdoers, if he could.

Just like that. No excess words, no waiting for any explanations or excuses. The son of a bitch! He felt like running up behind him and kicking him in the ass.

"And you don't have but forty-five more minutes to finish up, so you better get a move on!" Simon growled out over his shoulder as he walked under the exit sign, heading for the seventeenth floor.

The throbbing in the back of his head and the rage he felt at being treated like a child clashed inside his brain, made him feel helpless.

"Nigger!" he screamed when he was certain that Simon was halfway to the next floor.

"Niggggerrrr!" He rolled the word off his tongue as he reached for the buffer handle.

"Nigggerrrrr," he rolled out again, praying inside that

Simon hadn't heard him. There was no way he could think of out-thumping him. No way.

His mellow mood returning, he slowly turned Simon out. "Ol' Unca Tom ass motherfucker," he mumbled viciously to himself, in the process of doing a sloppy job on the next two floors. What could you expect from a chump who didn't want to do, didn't *know* how to do anything but work for a living?

Stupid sonofabitch! they put his head in a vise about forty-five years ago, squeezed all the "sensible" juices out of it and refilled it with whatever they felt was necessary ... to get him to obey the commands.

Here Spot! fetch Simon! attaboy Spot! down Simon! eat Spot! sic 'em Simon! here Simon! fetch Spot! chase the car wheels, Spot-Simon! Yeahhhh, that's what made the difference between the squares and the other kind of people. The squares took their programming lightly, it put no problem on their heads at all. None at all, they just did what they were supposed to do.

Elijah fumbled through the keys on his custodian's key chain for the key to the equipment room. Stashing the buffer inside, in its proper place, underneath the shelves of toilet paper, scouring powder and soap, the thought swept through his mind. I bet Li'l Bit, Blue, Sneezy and the rest of the neighborhood dopefiends would pay to have these keys. The thought was still circling around in his head as he made his way down to Simon's fifth floor office.

He dropped the keys on Simon's desk and eased out into the hallway. Five minutes to twelve. This was the part he hated most of all. No matter how soon you finished up, you still had to drop your keys off in Simon's office and wait until he dismissed you, at exactly twelve o'clock.

Elijah nodded to the dudes he felt some cohesion with, ignored all the others, the Simon types.

"Awright everybody, twelve o'clock," Simon announced from his office. Elijah strolled toward the exit, frowning. Asshole! He was worse than one of those ol' time cotton field strawbosses, the kind the Great White Father used to have keeping all the rest of the hands in line. The H.N.I.C.

"Brookes! hold up! I wanna talk to you for a minute!"

The rest of the men, glad to be free of the humdrum, split past Elijah as though they were two sections of a stream and he a rock in the middle.

He had the impulse, watching Simon lock his office door, to scream at him, "Hurry up, asshole! you makin' me miss the summertime!" But, instead, he waited patiently, determined to be cool.

"You know, you ain't such a bad guy as you pretend to be, Brookes . . . if you would go 'head 'n do your work when you was supposed to, and do as good a job as you can, you wouldn't have no trouble outta me. None at all."

Elijah listened to Simon's slow, rumbling voice down five flights of stairs, looking across and up at the man, from time to time. Be a good nigger . . . that's all you saying to me, sho' will be . . . when hell freezes over!

"Just think about what I said, Brookes," Simon concluded as they walked through the lobby, past the two senior citizen security guards.

"Yeahhh, I'll sho' 'nuff be doin' that, bruh Simon," Elijah purred at him. Throw the mark out a home plate by slinging a bucket of honey at his head.

Simon blinked, surprised at the pleasant response he'd gotten from his lecture. Never could tell about guys like Brookes.

Elijah waved at Simon as a last, pleasant gesture and turned the corner of Jackson and State, heading for a midnight lakefront walk. Time to think, time to start trying to pick up the pieces, to start trying to figure out another game. One month of stomp down labor was too goddamned much to take.

Elijah sat at the bar of the Tiger Lounge, casually flirting with the daytime bartender, glad that he didn't have to avoid seeing any of the regulars.

"Why don't you stir your finger around in my drink, baby . . . ?"

"What would that do?" she asked him, sliding a rum 'n Coke across to him.

"Well, it would make it taste better, for one thing."

"Honey, if I stuck my finger in your drink, it would taste too good to drink . . . that'll be one twenty-five."

He slid a couple singles off of his slim roll, trying to ignore the lady's cynical look. "Here you go, keep the change, sweet finger."

"Thanks, big timer," she replied in a cold, detached voice, and turned back to polishing glasses.

Rotten bitch, he decided casually, despite her big bumblebee ass and the cross-slashed blouse that took him past a breast outline and a nipple tip, overlaid by a piece of finely woven fishnet.

He hunched himself over his drink, staring at the bartender's buttocks, at the arrangement of tables and chairs behind him in the wall mirror across from him remembering all the scheming he had done sitting at one of those tables or another, and back to the bartender's buttocks grinding, shifting, tempting him. Yeahhh, the bitch can tell I ain't into too much from the fact that I'm up in here in the daytime. And from my garments.

He casually looked down at his shirt and pants. Wowww. I bet I look just like any plain ol' working dude. He had half an urge to ease off the stool, to somehow evade the putdown feeling he had, but decided to stick it out, through his drink anyway.

Bitch! he cursed the bartender in his mind for making him feel like a chump . . . a mark . . . a pootbutt. Funny, it never seemed to be anything but feast or famine. Never an in between thing. Either too much or too little. Browney. That cold-blooded white . . .

"How 'bout doin' this again, sweet finger?"

Elijah watched the lady go through her motions, not caring what she thought of him, what his image was, as he paid her the price of the drink and offered no tip.

Brooding over his current lightweight situation and how he was going to improve it prevented him from noticing Bro' Toe easing up to his side.

"Elijah! heyyyyy blood! wha's happenin'? I heard you was back on the set. Where you been keepin' yourself?"

Elijah took the figure standing at his side in, in sections. The expensive hat, the matching nowadays outfit, the Other kind of footwear, favored by those who could prove by wearing them that they didn't have to run from anybody. Made the way they were, it would've been impossible anyway.

"Oh heyyy Toe, what's goin' on?" Elijah responded, trying to sound supercasual.

Toe plopped down on the stool next to him, exposing his manicure and his pinkie ring to their best lights.

"Where you been keepin' yourself?" Toe asked again, as though he really wanted to know.

Elijah stared into his glass for a long minute. Where have I been keeping myself?

"I got a thang goin' on, over on the Westside," he answered vaguely.

Toe, playing soft con, deliberately looked Elijah over, from head to foot, making it very obvious that he was doing exactly that. "Tough, huh? I mean, gettin' it back together again."

Elijah took a long pull on his drink. Why bullshit the Toe? he was hip to the hustler's ups 'n downs. "Well, you know how it is. Ain't the first time I've had to start from scratch."

"If you got some scratch to start with," Toe added.

"Yeahhh, if you got some scratch to start with," Elijah mumbled in a monotone.

Toe dug down into his pocket and peeled two twenties off of a fat roll under the log's edge. "Here, man," he whispered out of the corner of his mouth, "pay me when you git it. Cool? Uhhh . . . whatchu into? anything heavy?"

Elijah carefully folded the money and stuffed it into his pocket. Who in the fuck refuses money? 'cept in the movies.

"I got a gig, Toe," he replied drily, the second rum 'n Coke loosening him up.

Toe straightened up, the perfect picture of someone completely surprised by something he had heard. "You got a what?" he asked.

"You heard me," Elijah replied in a low voice. "I got a gig, a yoke, a slave, a job."

Toe began to laugh, ignoring the bartender-lady's bright smile and attentive stance in front of them. He laughed, at first because of the absurdity of what he had heard, and after a few seconds, because it was really funny to him.

Elijah felt tempted to laugh himself. It *was* funny.

Wiping tears out from the corners of his eyes, with his pinkie cuttin' up, Toe turned semi-serious. "You wouldn't be jivin' me, would you, man?"

"I sure in fuck wish I was."

The bartender leveled a glancing smile and twelve feet of cleavage at the Toe as she scooted away to deal with two people at the end of the bar.

"Yeahhh, well, we was wonderin' what had happened to you down at the Stickhall. I asked Sid about you the other day. Seriously, you actually workin'?"

"Uh huh."

Toe made a grand motion with his right hand, summoning the bartender-lady.

"We'll have another of whatever my friend is drinkin' 'n a double Johnny Red on the stones for me, bring 'em on over to the table, will ya, baby?"

Elijah gulped the rest of his drink and allowed Toe to steer him by the elbow, over to the table section. He gestured away from the back booth. "Anywhere but back there. I got bad vibes about the whole area."

Toe smiled, remembering the bust. "Yeahhh, I remember that spot too." He settled them at a table against the far wall, gave the bartender, now turned shit eatin' waitress for a two-dollar tip, to place their drinks on the table. "Yeahhh, I sho' 'nuff remember that spot. You know I had 'bout six ounces o' shit pinned between my legs the night they busted you?"

Elijah took a sip of his drink. What was there to say? Maybe the next time would be the Toe's turn.

"What's happenin' with Murph and Jackson?"

"Oh, they still fuckin' with people whenever they want to, you know how it is."

The two men stirred their drinks simultaneously, each of them aware that the other one had something to lay on the other one . . . in due course.

"Uhh, what's happenin' with Bennie?"

Elijah allowed a disdainful look to sweep across his face. "Last time I saw Bennie, a couple brothers was spreadin' some o' his shit on they dicks."

"Really?! that's too bad."

"Yeah, well, you know how it is, if you can't hold your mug. But hey, man . . . I don't want to talk about Bennie. What's on your mind?"

Toe slugged his double down and signalled for a fresh round. "Mannnnn." He leaned in close, takin' care business-time. "Dig, I'm into a dynamite scene. It's called the pots 'n pans game."

Elijah found his smile giving way to a belly laugh before

he had a chance to control it. Pots 'n pans?!

"Uhhh, go 'head, Toe . . . I'm sorry, man . . . it just struck me funny for a minute. Pots 'n pans?"

"I can dig it," the Toe leaned back to slide his hand down the bartender's back before paying for their drinks.

"Anything else?" she asked, trying to get deeper into Toe's roll.

"Not just now, baby . . . maybe later."

She nudged his shoulder with her left breast making change and graciously accepted the three-dollar tip.

Elijah took it all in. The play. A slight smile still on his lips. Pots, pans, buffers. Shit! the next thing would be kitchen cleanser and house cleaning.

"Okay, dig, Elijah . . . lemme run it down to you. I may as well tell you right now, I *know* that you gon' wanna get in on this . . ."

Elijah leaned in closer, glancing into Toe's eyes, from time to time, checking out the pulse vein on the side of his throat, watching his hands as he talked, paying close attention to all the things that might tell him whether or not the bullshitter was trying to bullshit the bullshitter.

CHAPTER 7

Elijah allowed himself to get caught up in the afternoon, downtown, lunch hour crowd . . . maintaining his own un-hurried pace in the middle of the lemming movement.

He caught sight of himself in a store window and paused to admire his image. No hat because the Toe had explained that sometimes the ladies didn't trust dudes when they couldn't see all of him, like from top to bottom. But everything else was there, the very prosperous look of a successful operator. Now. With a hip little attache case yet.

He caught the reflection of the building he had worked in, up until a week ago, at the same time he caught sight of his prey dawdling along, trying to use up that ten or twelve minutes that she hadn't used up, rushing from her office building to a nearby coffee shop and back.

He locked his step into hers ten paces behind. Everything was timing. Timing was everything. If he hit at her too far away from her job she would feel threatened by a delay. If he approached her too close to her job and she was a priggy type, she might be terribly offended for appearances' sake, at the idea of a strange dude stopping her on the street.

For the hundreth time, he thought, too bad it's got to be sisters, but that's what the program calls for.

He appraised her body as he closed in. Beautiful li'l brown skinned sister, ass stuck out like it had a shelf under it, nice legs too, and a pretty face. Yeahhh . . .

He suaved himself up to her left shoulder and with a languid motion presented her his card, stopping her in her tracks as he instantly began to rap.

This was a delicate section of the game too. He knew, from past experiences, that he had to give her enough time to read the card but not enough time to think about it.

"Good afternoon, Miss" . . . nothing too flirty . . . "my name is Phillip Dobson, Regional Sales Representative for Astro Cookware Products. The card I've just handed you can be used for a discount on any Astro product. Now then, at this point, may I ask whether or not you're married?"

He carefully concealed his urge to strike a hip pose as she gave him the once over. He knew the look . . . it seemed as though they had stolen it directly from the faces of a thousand bargain-hunting white middle-aged women on a thousand daytime quiz shows.

"Well, no. Not yet. I'm engaged," she informed him, through white, even teeth and rosebud lips.

Ain't this somethin' . . . a sister talkin' 'bout she's "engaged." Why didn't she just come on out and say she 'n some dude is fuckin' regular. Lawwwd, I swear! my people!

"Beautiful! that's fine! Now, to make absolutely certain that you are eligible for Astro Cookware service, may I ask if you are twenty-four or younger? I can just about tell from lookin' at your pretty skin that you must be about that . . . am I right?"

"I'm twenty-two." She flashed her eyelashes at him and held her wristwatch up theatrically. "And I have to get back to work in a few minutes. Why?"

Elijah nodded his head in agreement and pulled the stopper out. "I'm glad you asked that question before I had a chance to give you an answer. Our company has taken a survey to determine the greatest household need of single black career women . . . like yourself . . . aged twenty-four and younger . . . who are, of course, plannin' to get married sometime. Or . . ." He paused for a really roguish wink. "Hah hah hah, set up housekeepin' of one sort or another.

"The one single item we have discovered, that is always necessary, aside from love and affection, is pots and pans. May sound incredible but it's the absolute truth. Now, we invite you to consider one thing seriously . . . your husband may support you. He may even do the cooking for you, even if it's only boiling an egg, but one thing is certain . . . you are definitely goin' to need cookware.

"Would you be kind enough to provide us with your name, address and telephone number? I would like to phone you, arrange to drop in, at your convenience, for a complete, no-obligation-to-buy demonstration of our Astro

Cookware."

Elijah held the ballpoint and contract out to her with complete assurance that she would sign on the dotted line, and she did. "Thank you, very much, Miss . . . uhhh . . . Sister Brown. Could you give me the best possible time to . . . uhhh?"

"Evenings, after six are the best times for me," she replied hurriedly and rushed to one of the stalagmites four doors away.

"We'll be callin' you, Sister Brown . . . tomorrow at the latest."

He flipped his attache case open and slid the contract inside. Women were so fuckin' gullible when they wanted to be, it seemed. Here's a chick working hard all day who'd sign her fuckin' life away, maybe . . . and not even suspect it.

Toe was right. A good appearance, a hard, clean, steady rap and the possibility . . . just the possibility of getting something for nothing was apt to make the average woman weak in the head.

He strolled north on State Street, looking for victims, watching the lunch hour crowds thin out. He allowed two possibles to slip by, feeling well fed and heavy about the ribs with five contracts already signed in his attache case.

Funny, he thought, walking into Field's air-conditioned, perfumed atmosphere, funny how even the most intelligent chicks will go for the most mediocre game. And those who won't go for it. Well, what the fuck! You can't win 'em all.

He wandered into the store's coffee shop for a cool drink. That was one of the drawbacks to the hustle, he felt . . . in the summertime you could get pretty thirsty.

Wonder what the wintertime would be like?

On his way back out into the streets, he spotted a victim behind the counter in the ladies' blouses. In a split second he had caught all the signs . . . in addition to the fact that she had looked at him one second too long with that open expression meaning, "I like . . ."

He approached her section from an oblique angle, slid up on her blind side and went into his act.

Three-fourths of the way through, he became aware that he was being monitored by the sister's white counterpart in their section . . . all green eyes and pursed lips.

Ten lines before the clincher, the sister was called away by an imperialistic-looking old dame in a motheaten fox fur.

"Excuse me, I've got a customer, be right back."

Elijah smiled graciously and placed his case on the counter, to re-shuffle his small list of names and addresses into alphabetical order, killing a few minutes.

He saw her move toward him out of the corner of his eye. "Pardon me, I couldn't help overhearing your conversation with Dot. I could use some cookware myself. Is your offer only limited to black females under twenty-four, and working?"

Elijah felt himself frowning before he had a chance to control his feelings about her southern accent. It was slight and flavored with something else, but he still didn't dig it.

"Is my offer limited to . . . ? Uhhh, no, not really. White women spend a li'l time in their own kitchens too, nowadays, don't they?" he responded slyly, glancing over at the sister wrangling with the fox fur.

"I always have," green eyes answered coolly.

131

"Okay, sign here and I'll bring a complete set to your home, at your convenience, all right?"

He shoved a dummy contract across the counter, feeling vaguely pissed because his time was being so misused.

"Don't I get a sales talk too, you know, your li'l song 'n dance?"

He refocussed. Where was this cracker bitch comin' from? He studied her for a hard minute. Green, sea-green eyes, black, black hair, dark, swarthy skin, no tan. Italian? Armenian? Greek? or something. Ripe body, she'll be fat in five years if she isn't careful.

Her direct look mocked him.

"Are you sure you need a song 'n dance?"

"Why not?" She laid an expansive gesture on him. "That's your job, isn't it?"

The fox fur was joined by a pair of rhinestone spectacles in dumpy slacks and two-toned platform shoes.

Elijah slid through his speech in a dry monotone, feeling vaguely trapped. At the conclusion, he slid the form back across to her.

Her smile was pure sarcasm. "My name is Clotille Montgomery and the whole deal sounds like a bummer to me. Not only that, I think I'm going to tell Dot not to get anything from you either."

Elijah felt the wildest urge to lean across the counter and crack her one on the jaw. Who in the hell did she think she was?

He decided to finesse his way through the situation. "You think you're strong enough to turn my thing around?"

"Uhh huh," she answered, her left eyebrow arched, challenging him.

He took stock of things. Yeahhh, she probably could badmouth things so bad that he wouldn't be able to get over. But there were lots of ways to skin a cat.

He slowly allowed his hundred-dollar-bill smile to open up on her. "You jivvvvvve ass . . ."

"You dirty, rotten . . ." she answered with equal strength. They stood toe to toe, a glass counter between them, the sounds of the store suspended, people suddenly far away.

Simultaneously, their smiles lapsed into grins.

"What time do you get off?"

"Five o'clock."

"I'll pick you up. Maybe I can get my black ass hung buyin' you a drink."

"Not unless I scream rape."

Elijah took another long, hard look at her, closed his case and eased away, slipping off of Sister Dot's blind side, knowing what she was going to think of him, what she was going to call him when she realized what he had been about. Or maybe Clotille would tell her.

He looked back at their section from across the store, camouflaged by a rack of ties in the men's wear department. She and Clotille had their heads together. What was the white bitch running down to the sister? Clotille Montgomery . . . with her semi-slick ass!

He strolled out of the store, the afternoon heat shimmering up from the concrete in hazy patterns, heading for the lakefront, wondering whether or not he should go home and change, or just hang around 'til five.

The bitch *was* fine. No doubt about it.

He began putting his program together as he walked. Make her wait fifteen minutes . . . or at least 'til the sister split. Stop downtown in one of the more cosmopolitan places for a taste and after that . . . after that, no telling . . . hop in a cab and head straight for the killin' floor or whatever.

Too bad she's a white broad, he decided as the first cool breeze from the lake hit him; if she wasn't, as game as she seems to be, we might be able to get off into something really positive. Really positive . . .

Elijah looked up and down the rows of pots and pans in the garage and smiled as he listened to Toe rap.

"Mannnn, you shoulda seen this honky's face when I told him, gimme a hundred o' them 'n a hundred o' those 'n a hundred o' these. By the time I finished layin' out a grand in his joint, he would've kissed my ass through a straw if I'd wanted 'im to."

Elijah nodded, calculating the number of pots and pans he had sold in the last month. "That's the way Whitey is, man . . . he'll do anything for money."

"Niggers will too, blood. Quiet as it's kept," Toe replied drily. "Okay, you've had close to six weeks at it. What do you think?"

Elijah started off cautiously. "Well . . . the dough is beautiful. The set up is made for me, but . . . hahhhah . . . I don't think my ol' bones is gon' be able to hold up under all this drippin' drama it's put me into."

Toe dug his hands down into his pockets and scratched his testicles indulgently. "Fringe benefits we call 'em. We got a dude out west . . ." He made a sly pause. "You 'member Nickodemus?"

Elijah answered with a straight face. Yeahhh, asshole, I know about him and Leelah. "Yeah, man, you know I used to hustle with Nick, what's he doin'?"

"Awww, we put him into a couple shoppin' plazas over there, somebody taught him how to say good mornin' and gimme some, in Spanish ... and now we don't even see the dude but once a week, when he comes over to give us his delivery sheet."

"It's a choice setup, Toe. Single, workin' broads under twenty-four ... like takin' candy from a baby. You know I haven't been home in a week? and I got a thang goin' on this evenin'."

"Hahhh hahhh hahhah ... that's what happened to Nick, with them Puerto Rican chicks out west."

Elijah allowed himself a tight little laugh with the Toe. The situation *was* sweet ... legitimately selling cheap sets of cookware to a herd of gullible young chicks for three times the price that they would pay in the store. And with a legitimate contract that said they knew that, and had to pay for what they got, anyway. The really hip thing about it all was that only one out of ten even thought about trying to default after they found out the truth, the rest feeling so sold by the seller that they seemed to feel ashamed to balk. Or maybe they felt honor bound to fulfill an obligation, even a bad one.

Elijah stepped through the smaller door cut into the garage face behind Toe. "You know, I been meanin' to ask you, Toe ... about the operation. When you be sayin' we this 'n we that ... who is 'we?' "

Toe snapped the paddlock on the door and stabbed Elijah with a sour look. "You gettin' yours, ainchu?"

"Right on, bruh . . . right on! but I was just wonderin', you know? who this 'we' was, that you . . . ?"

Toe pulled at the lock again, to make certain that it was securely in place. "I'm surprised at you, blood. You know who 'we' is, the same fuckin' 'we' that it's always been. You want a lift somewhere?"

Elijah nodded yes and followed Toe to his alley-long Fleetwood . . . reminding himself to be cool and not create waves, not for a while, anyway.

Elijah jumped out of the cab and walked slowly under the awning leading to the foyer of Clotille's apartment building.

The doorman of the building, a medium-sized, middle-aged black man with upturned Irish features, looked at him reproachfully. After a few visits, he knew who Elijah was going to see and his whole attitude showed jealous disapproval.

Elijah stood in front of the door that was customarily opened for the white tenants and their white visitors. So far as anyone knew, no obviously black person lived there.

"Well, I guess you ain't gon' open the door for me, huh?"

"Open your own goddamned doors!" the doorman snapped at him and glared off into the distance.

Elijah laid a mercilessly evil grin on him, opened the door as though it weighed three thousand pounds, walked over to the intercom setup and prepared to announce himself.

By Odie Hawkins

"Hey, you ain't supposed to be usin' that!" the doorman said to him, following him.

"I know, man, but if you ain't gon' do your job just because . . ."

The doorman snatched the intercom telephone off its hook and buzzed Clotille's apartment. "There's a man down here to see you, Mizz Montgomery."

"Tell 'er it's the nigger she loves," Elijah egged the scene on. The doorman, a black snob's snob from 'way back, snapped his head around and glared at Elijah. "What's your name, fella?"

"E. Phillip Dobson the First, Mr. Phillip Dobson the First." He spoke in a louder voice than necessary, teasing the man.

"Man named Dobson, Mizz Montgomery . . . uhh . . . yes, m'am."

Elijah sneered . . . "Yes m'am" . . . woww, talk about Stone Age types!

The doorman took his own sweet time opening up the door to the lobby. Elijah looked at the side of the man's face on his way in and, for a split second, felt pity and then hate.

As the heavy door slowly resettled itself, Elijah spoke quickly. "If it wasn't for Unca' Tom ass dudes like you, niggers wouldn't be havin' such a tough time tryin' to get over today!"

The doorman hurriedly reopened the door and shouted across the expensively carpeted lobby. "If it wasn't for Uncle Tom ass dudes like me, niggers like you wouldn't be havin' a chance to eat all the chalk pussy you want, or nothin' else, for that matter!"

Elijah felt like running back across the lobby and thumpin' the old dude's ass, but for what? and besides it would be a total waste of good cocaine feeling.

He stood in front of the elevator, steaming. Talk about bad vibes . . . wowww! He stared at the doorman's back as the elevator slid from the twelfth floor. Yeahhh, I can dig where you comin' from, ol' dude. Been doin' the best you know how, for as long as you can remember, and all of a sudden, just when it seems to be settling into some kind of groove, along comes one of these slick ass, upstart motherfuckers to steal all of the pussy from you, even the smell . . . after all these years of Yes M'amin' 'n No Suhhin', prayin' that somebody would leave you a few grand or so in they wills. Or at least give you a feel. He stepped into the carpeted elevator, feeling good about having figured it all out, and kept his cool.

Clotille leaned against the wall outside her apartment, a drink in one hand, a joint in the other hand, half high *and* half drunk.

Elijah frowned, glancing at the other apartment doors as he walked to her, trying not to look anxious. Damn! this is all I need . . . a fucked up white bitch outside in the hall with a joint, in a building way out here on the Other side, where even the nigger doorman hates niggers.

"Well, *Mr.* Phillip Dobson the First, I see you finally made it, only an hour and a half late this time."

Her Southern-proper-lady voice, mounted by a boozy slur, grated in his ears. "I had some business to take care of, baby . . . you know how it be."

"Yeahhh, yeahhh, I know how it *be!* That's the same routine you've given me about ten times in the last two weeks."

Cooling it, he strolled past her into the apartment, headed straight for the bamboo bar across the room, mixed himself a gin 'n tonic. Fuck mint juleps tonight! and sprawled on the sofa, a Danish job splattered with wild semen shots.

Clotille straggled in after him, trying to contain her anger, and got about the business of mixing herself another one. She came over to stand in front of him, alternately sucking on the joint and sipping her drink.

"Clo' . . . ?"

"I was goin' to try to fix you some kind of dinner," she interrupted him, her green eyes reddened, "but when I finally got around to tryin' to cook in some of my 'stainless' Astro cookware, the damned paint started peeling off the bottom of the pot."

Elijah almost choked on his drink, laughing.

"What the hell's so funny, damn it!"

He straightened up, the cocaine he had snorted in the cab freezing his nose in little ripples. "You are, baby-sweets . . . you are. I woulda waited for ice water in hell just to see the look on your face after you'd found out that your would-be-slick-ass had been rooked."

Clotille slid down onto the sofa beside him, flashing a bare knee and thigh through the slit in her robe. "You're a devil, you know that?"

"I been called worse."

"Well, at any rate, I want my money back."

"What fuckin' money back?! Shit! you signed a contract,

a no-money-back guarantee. If you don't believe me, check your contract out. And besides, what's two hundred to you?''

Clotille slopped half her drink onto the coffee table in front of them and placed the half-smoked roach in an ashtray. "What's *that* supposed to mean?"

Elijah retrieved the joint from the ashtray and took a couple deep hits before answering. "Heyyyy, what do I look like to you? Some new kind o' fool!? Do you think I could believe for a minute that you could live in a joint like this, wear the kind o' garments you wear and drive the kind o' ride you got, on a salesgirl's pay? huh?"

An ugly smile slid onto Clotille's mouth. "What else do you *think* you know about me?"

"What else do you want me to tell you? About how you decided to come down out of your ivory tower and see how the other half was livin'?"

"You really think you know every damned thing, don't you? Well, let me tell you a thing or two, *Mr. Dobson!*"

Elijah watched her closely as she swayed up from the sofa and staggered over to the bar to fix herself a fresh drink. He shook his head sadly, thinking . . . funny about white folks, lots of 'em . . . they got everything they need, ain't hurtin' for nothing, lots of 'em, and yet they wind up being more fucked up than people who ain't got shit and ain't never had shit.

Especially the women. Look at this bitch up in here . . . a three hundred 'n fifty-dollar-a-month apartment, at least . . . money from a trust fund set up by a cotton plantation daddy. Cotton plantation! The whole concept of her money coming from a cotton plantation had almost blown him away.

He had gotten her into a drunken stupor one night and pumped her . . . and after that, and a dumb, animal, drunken-two-people orgy, he had searched through enough papers to find out the whole business of her life. Family albums and captions were a dead giveaway.

"Phillip, are you listenin' to me!?" she screamed across the room.

"Yeah, I'm listenin' to you," he replied absently.

"Yes, it's true, about what you're sayin', about me havin' money. But about my daddy havin' money . . . money! moneyyy!"

He watched her carefully, recognizing the fact that she had reached the fucked-up point, and that beyond that would be no sense . . . or worse.

"Yeah, sure, he had, has money . . . and I could continue to be a parasite if I wanted to. Are you trying to see how the other half is living by being a parasite?"

The way she said it made him angry enough to leave, or kick her ass. He placed his glass on the table and stood up to leave.

"Where're you goin'?" she asked him, her voice almost caricaturing a black dialect.

"You think I wanna sit here 'n listen to all this bullshit?" he blustered back at her, not really sure of why he wanted to split, feeling a little fucked up himself, behind the girl, the drink and the smoke.

"Yeahhhh, you think I'm gon' sit here . . . what the hell do you think I care 'bout how hard you had it, you knew you didn't have to . . . not after you realized you was free, white and yo' da da was gonna wipe your ass whenever it needed it."

He heard his words and felt, somehow, that they were a continuation of some argument they had had, from some other time.

"That's the kind of thinkin' that will keep you down in the ghetto, just another li'l black hustler!" she shot back at him, also going back to an earlier "discussion," both of them feeling slightly nutted out on their highs.

"You neurotic white punk bitch!"

He was across the room, slamming his fists to her head and jaw before the word was fully released. "Nigggg . . . !" A few wild chops cut her down. He stood over her feeling murderous.

"Oohhh, my God! I didn't mean . . . I didn't mean to call you anything wrong . . . I'm sorry . . . sorry . . . sorry . . ."

He looked down into her pleading eyes, hating her. "Bitch! The nerve of you! callin' me a nigger. I oughta stomp your ass into the ground!"

Clotille groveled on the rug around his pants cuffs, a caricature of a woman begging for absolution. "Phillip, please forgive me . . . I didn't mean . . ."

He stumbled, pulling his leg out of her grasp, walked to the door and turned to spit on the floor before opening it. "That's what I think of you!" he said coldly and walked out scowling.

Outside in the corridor, he leaned his ear against the door to listen to her drunken sobs, feeling pleased with himself about it all, about how quickly he had handled things.

He had double feelings, heading toward the elevator . . . one part of him aroused by her pathetic sounds and the treatment he knew she would give him if he went back. But his head prevailed. She would be more and more a problem as time went on because that's where they had been headed from the beginning . . . his vibes had told him that, and besides, she was a Taurus.

Waiting for the elevator, a developing erection flashed his mind back and forth, from going back down the hallway to Clotille to paying Ramona Brown a visit. Ramona, he decided, that's what I need, a li'l soul work . . .

He didn't pay the woman much attention as she stood beside him, waiting for the elevator . . . just another middle-aged, trying-to-be-young white woman with a crinkly tan.

She crinkled her mouth into a patronizing smile as she hesitantly stepped into the elevator with him. "Are you delivering something in the building?" she asked.

"Yeah, I'm delivering bad, black vibrations. You want some?"

She shook her head unconsciously and stared at the wooden panels in the elevator with the dull look of someone who had been severely shocked.

"And you too, ol' jiveass, Unca' Tom son of a bitch!"

He called back to the doorman, watching him kowtow to the white woman as he walked down the street, looking for a cab, on his way to Sister Brown's house.

He felt her eyes on his face even before he was fully awake. Which one was this? he asked himself as he slowly fluttered his eyes open.

Ramona. Yeah, right. Now I remember. Fucked up, being stopped by the pigs over on the Other side, taken to the nearest bus stop. A bus to 35th Street and then a cab to Ramona's.

He stared at her. Five feet, two inches tall, coffee 'n cream colored, one hundred and fifteen delicious pounds, unmarried, under twenty-four years old and square as a brick.

"Phil?"

Elijah frowned slightly, a bad, thick taste in his mouth. Phil? Oooh yes . . . I *am* Phillip Dobson. God! I bet this young bitch would die if she found out that she had been screwin' a dude whose name wasn't even what she thought it was . . . either that or she'd go nuts.

"Hmmmmmmm?" he mumbled, sliding his left leg across both of her lush thighs.

"You know . . . my boyfriend is really mad at me."

Elijah reached over to the bedside table for a cigarette, decided to smoke the rest of the joint they had started on last night. Nothing better than starting off the day high. Wonder where she gets this dynamite?

"Why?" he asked, holding his second deep hit in.

"Well . . . he wanted to see me on Friday, but you said you were coming over, so I cancelled him out . . . but you didn't show up."

"Had somethin' to do, baby. You know how that is." He spoke softly and blew a stream of smoke into her face.

"Then he called me at work yesterday to ask me if he could see me tonight . . . but I didn't know if you were coming over, so . . . I . . . uhh . . ."

144

Elijah cocked a hot eye at her bare breasts. "Wh
you all supposed to be gettin' married?"

"Next month," she answered shyly, pulling the cover up
over her breasts.

Elijah stubbed the joint out and slid down in bed, pulling her with him.

"Heyyyy, baby," he reassured her, feeling a slight resistance. "I can't git it all. There'll be enough left for that
young fool. I'm just seasonin' it up a li'l bit for 'im."

She buried her face in the muscles of his chest and
sighhhed. "Phil, you just make me feel terrible . . . just
terrible."

He smiled down on her perma-straightened head. Yeah,
I just bet I do . . .

CHAPTER 8

Elijah blew a long whistle of amazement to discover that there was a parking space practically in front of the Afro Lounge . . . known up until two weeks before as the Tiger Lounge.

The sign in the window said in bold, florid letters, "Under New Management," but Elijah and the other regulars knew that there was no new management, the owner's ol' lady had just simply gotten tired of calling the place the Tiger Lounge and had decided to go for something she felt would be more relevant.

He made certain that the fast ladies tripping around outside the club and all of the telegraphers spotted him as he was parking his car. It was two years late but filled with gleaming fixtures and stuffed with imitation black panther upholstery.

The Toe was responsible for him having it, clearing the deck with someone to make certain he was riding, at half the price someone else would have had to pay. "A dude who can sell like you, bruh . . . oughta be in the saddle."

Elijah had added gangster whitewalls and now he was on the scene, stylin' for the people who could really dig such things.

He took his time to lock the door and to double-check his defense system, installed primarily to prevent dope fiends and others from ripping his tapes and cassettes off.

He straightened up and turned to face the flickering neon lights, on stage, his stage. The street vibes and the Bolivian cocaine in his nostrils told him it was Saturday night and all was well.

His timing was excellent. They were all there, even the ones he had wanted to see when he first returned to the set, but couldn't. Yeahhhh, they were all there, waiting for him, it seemed to him . . . staring down at the twisted faces, the smiling faces, the ugly faces, the pretty faces, the faces of all the people he had been seeing in dreams and nightmares, ever since he had decided to do his thang.

"Bruh 'Lijah, c'mon on over here, lemme spend some o' this dirty money on buying you a drink!" Precious Percy, the pimp, called out to him, admiring his stance in the door, recognizing coke macho. Elijah slowly strutted along the length of the bar to a stool beside Precious, nodding coolly to the people he felt some cohesion with.

Precious ordered drinks and turned to Elijah, loaded himself. "You oughta come on into my line o' work, bruh . . . you were cut out for it, and believe me, I wouldn't say that to one nigger in a thousand . . . 'course, I have to admit that ho's ain't quite what they used to be . . ."

"Too much strain 'n pain, Precious. I'm havin' enough trouble tryin' to keep my shit together, freelance . . . and besides, I couldn't take the hours."

Precious laughed quietly and shrugged. "Yeahhh, I hear ya, brotherman, I hear ya."

Sid the Shark paused between the two men, checking out the action out of the corner of his eye. "What the fuck you two slick ass motherfuckers plottin'?"

Both of them turned smiles on him . . . Sid was not one to be casually out on Saturday night, his thing was business, business and more business.

"Heyyy, Sid, what's goin' on?"

"Yeahhh, what's happenin', Sid?"

Sid roved his pouchy, foxy eyes all over a trio of dazzling young female bodies at a nearby table before answering. "I got my hands full . . . tryin' to keep these young fools away from what's righteously mine."

Percy and Elijah exchanged winks, following Sidney's gaze; if there was one thing the Shark really loved, it was young pussy.

He drifted away as Nick and Leelah strolled in; Nick, catching sight of Elijah before Leelah did, looked away nervously. Elijah smiled maliciously in their direction.

"See. Now that's the kind of shit that makes your job hard."

Precious nodded at the sight of two women in a gossip session on the sidewalk. He paid for the drinks and started out. "I'll catch you in a li'l bit, blood . . . I gotta git out here 'n shake this young bitch up."

"Got somethin' new?" Elijah asked, checking out the scene beyond the plate glass and the neon.

"I keep somethin' new, that's the name of the game."

Elijah studied the reaction of the two women as they saw Precious Percy walk out of the bar. The one who didn't belong to him immediately eased across the street in a rush.

As though it were a scene from a play in pantomime, the young, inexperienced prostitute's eyes wobbled in fright.

The blow, a hard, fast, right hook caught her under the left ear. Elijah involuntarily grimaced with vicarious pain.

Percy grabbed her under the armpits and forced her to stand up, mouthing quick, precise instructions as he did so. Elijah knew, from having heard it many times before, that Precious Percy the Pimp was re-stating the ground rules.

He finished his drink and decided to move on, to make an entrance at some other joint. He turned slowly on the bar stool to stare coldly at Leelah and Nick, seated at one of the tables on the other side of the room. What the hell, he thought, why create a scene? when you move you lose.

Nick wet his lips and struck up a sudden conversation with a couple at the next table. Leelah stared back defiantly.

Elijah slid off the stool and made a grand exit, his head smoky, his chest out, his cool intact.

Percy strolled over to him as he walked out of the door, massaging his knuckles.

"She shapin' up, Precious?" Elijah asked, knowing that the eyes of the players inside were checking them out.

"She'll be awright in a couple nights, or else she'll be on a train to Montana, or . . . somewhere."

149

"Tough titty . . ." Elijah started off, holding out both palms for the five-soul spank.

"But we needs the milk." Precious finished off the sentence and gave Elijah double fives.

"Oh . . . if you see Nick 'n Leelah inside, with sweat beads runnin' down the sides of they faces, tell 'em the big E said hello, willya?"

Precious allowed a brief smile to coat his mouth, enjoying the flavor of the lightweight intrigue. "Right on, blood . . . you gettin' on, huh?"

"Yeahhh," Elijah winked, "I got some business to take care."

"I hear ya, man . . . later."

"Yeahhh, later on, Precious."

Elijah popped into his 'chine and started driving, his moods alternating between high and low.

The lights of the Southside purred, flickered to him, made him park his car a few times and wander in and out, under their invitations.

A drink in the Living Room, the last of the cocaine in the men's room of the Matador Club, the powder almost slipping from his thumbnail as two drunks pushed their way into the narrow toilet. A flirtatious conversation with a forty-year-old housewife, out in the family station wagon, trying to get a little bit of what she had been hearing about for ten years of dull, married life. The Singapore for a funny-named drink and some greasy wonton, more flirtation, this time with a couple gays from California . . . what the hell, if it wasn't for ass, where would pussy be?

Two a.m., the after hours set at Livin' Swell's place.

"I know all you motherfuckers is jealous o' me."

"Why man?" someone was obligated to ask, a line that always had to be recited at some point, on Saturday night, in Livin' Swell's place.

"Why? 'cause I'm livin' swell, that's why," the fat man blew on cue and kept tending bar, charging a quarter more per drink because it was after hours, and he needed all the money he could make, to keep on livin' swell.

Listening to the developing roar of the crowd as the horses headed into the stretch, and the old gowster's tall, sad story of what the old days used to be like was exciting, disturbing, interesting. He glanced up at the board and casually ripped his lost bet in half. Another dog.

"Ain't havin' too much luck, huh, junior?" The old gowster pinned him with a shrewd look.

Elijah glared at the old dude postured in front of him, half man, half facade, all hustler, and smiled. Yeahhh, to him, at fifty odd, having played all games, everybody was junior something or other.

"You know how it is, you win some, you lose a few."

The old timer swallowed his sarcastic reply and looked over both shoulders, as though suspecting a hand would snatch him away. "Uhhh, say, looka here, junior . . . I wonder if you might be able to slap a slat on me? I got a hot tip on this next one."

Elijah leaned back on the kidney-shaped sofa, watching Toe divide a medium-sized pyramid of cocaine into six thick lines, fifteen hundred dollars in his pocket. The smile

151

on his face stemmed from and covered the memory of the last five races. What had happened after he had loaned (given, actually) the ol' hustler (what'shisname?) ten dollars?

In a word, everything! he decided; at least it came to one grand and a half. A lot to smile about. Luck? why not call it that?

Toe's lady, a half something and half something else, with eyes like a cat's and stacked stone to the bone wandered through, fluffing up the pillows on the sofa across from them. Toe nodded her out of the room and handed Elijah a strawed-up twenty-dollar bill. "Here you go, blood."

Elijah bent over the low, Afro-Danish coffee table in front of them and snorted a line up each nostril.

Toe did the same thing and called out, as though he were signalling to a favorite pet. "Hassani, com'mere!"

She reappeared from one of the other rooms, billowing in in a see-through caftan, her reddish-black hair streaming down behind. Was she an Arab? No wonder Toe was sitting up in blood-red polka-dot drawers and undershirt.

She held her hair gracefully off to one side and bent over to snort two lines. Elijah tried to keep his eyes on some neutral spot in the room as she flowed away.

"Go 'head, man . . . the last two is yours."

Elijah bent back over the table, feeling as though cold wire brushes were being brushed across the bridge of his nose, a zing feeling.

The last two lines froze the zing feeling, slowed it down. When he held his head back up, he had the sensation that he was sitting up straighter than he had ever sat in his life.

"So, you wanna cut us loose, huh?"

He had to pinch his nostrils together a few times, to somehow control the zing feeling that had now turned into a dry ice cube oozing down the back of his throat. Goddamn! talk about coke! This shit must be almost pure girl.

"Well, like I told you before, man . . . I wanted a stake, you know, to get the front I needed. You gave me that and I'm grateful . . . but now it's time for me to get down with my very own thang."

"Yeah, I hear ya, bruh . . . I hear ya, whatchu got in mind?"

Elijah looked around the room, collecting himself. "Oh, I got a couple or three ideas."

Toe responded with a sly look on his face, his eyes widened by the coke. "That's cool. You don't have to run it down to me. I know it must be somethin' really groovy if you wanna cut the pots 'n pans thang loose."

"Well, you know how it is . . . if you used to doin' your own thang . . . besides, the pots 'n pans scene is too much like work."

Toe burst into hysterical laughter for a full minute, leaving Elijah to wonder whether or not he was laughing at what he had just said, or whether he was just laughing period.

"Yeah, I can dig it! I can dig it! run it down to me? Hassani, come get somethin' on the TV!" Toe ran things together, forgetting that he had just absolved Elijah from explaining what his new deal might be.

The coke in Elijah's head made him stare boldly at the full moon split of Hassani's behind as she bent over to adjust the huge color television set a few feet across from

153

them.

"You don't want the sound, do you?" she asked without looking around.

"Nawww, just the picture. Ain't she got a helluva ass on 'er?"

Toe's question jarred Elijah slightly. "Uhhh . . . right on!"

As she eased away from in front of the screen, the colored images flickering in front of their faces pulled them both into the tube. Elijah blinked his eyes with the clarity of what he was seeing. Who was the black dude on the screen raising hell in front of all those people? Who was he?

"Motherfucker sho' got a big mouth, ain't he?"

Toe broke the spell.

The militant young dude in front of the store . . . the day he and Nick had been out doing the short change game? Yeahhh, the same one. He must really be serious.

"I been checkin' into the black, black thing," Elijah started off slowly, his eyes glued to the figure on the screen.

"Yeah?"

"Yeah, you know, Afro pride 'n shit. There's a lot o' dough to be made in all that. 'Member Wimpy?"

"Wimpy the junkie?"

"Uh huh, Wimpy the junkie. I got word in the joint that Wimpy had gotten hisself together, got somebody to write him up a proposal, sent it to some government office and would up with twenty-five grand to set up an anti-drug rehab program . . . twenty-five grand!"

"Yeahhh, yeahhh, that's happenin' these days. When they ain't throwin' niggers in concentration camps, they givin' money to set up en-counter groups 'n shit . . . to try to keep everybody cooled out."

"Well, you know how it is. A game is a game," Elijah added, and watched Hassani cross the room to bring Toe a drink. Damn! that bitch is fine.

"You wanna taste?" Toe asked in a sly voice, judging Elijah's thoughts from the look in his eyes.

Elijah slid his eyes away from Hassani's body. That's the kind of woman I needs . . . a real together, stomp down, nitty gritty lady.

"Uhh, nawwww, bruh Toe . . . I got to be gettin' on. We got all our shit squared away?"

Toe shrugged, a hip, philosophical curl at the edges of his mouth. "Everything's cool," Toe responded. Elijah stood up . . . 'way, 'way up . . .

"It's been real, man," he said and solemnly shook hands with Toe, noticing that he had a semi-erection.

"Right on, blood," Toe replied, winked and juggled his nuts with his free hand.

Elijah let loose a low, meant-to-be-dirty laugh, in tune with the moment, and glided out of Toe's apartment, the sexy vibes making him anxious to get off onto his set. Ramona, look out bayyy-bee, here I commme.

Elijah followed Ramona, pinkie fingers linked, through six stiff, cold, correct introductions in a row before he begged off, whispering into her ear that he had to go take a piss. She reluctantly excused him, her bottom lip pouted.

Bitches! he muttered viciously in the back of his mind . . . you long stroke 'em a few times and they think they own you. He groped his way through the black cocktail-whiskey 'n soda-everything-now crowd and fumbled into one of the four toilets in the house.

Standing above the seat, taking a few dribbling shots at the blue-tinted water in the stool, listening to Aretha outside, his dick firmly clenched between thumb and forefinger, he found himself watching a quiet, cold-blooded erection develop and collapse. Ain't really nobody here to fuck, he reflected, and composed himself to re-enter a world filled with Ramona Browns . . . blacks who had pulled off the supreme contradiction.

Two banana skin-colored, middle-aged women, modishly dressed, swished past him into the toilet as he made his exit. Jiveass booshiee bitches . . . either gossiping about some dumb chump one of them digs, or slipping a lick to each other's pussy on the sly . . . who knows?

He scooped a glass of cold duck from a waiter's passing tray and stood off to one side of a long hallway, checking out the action. A bunch of superficial assholes, he decided after a few minutes of careful study. Grating against the sound of soul music, their metallic, nazalized voices irritated him, made him feel that he wanted to jump on top of something and scream, "Awright! three or four of you wall-eyed spooks done got a degree or two or somethin' but it don't mean shit! y'all still just niggers! like me!"

He absent-mindedly dug down into his leather vest pocket for a home-rolled joint, thought about it for a split second and short-circuited himself. Wowwww! these motherfuckers don't even get loaded! They'd probably call the law on me if I fired one up.

He had noticed the absence of smoke in the house, of all

kinds, and had come across a hand-lettered sign on a coffee table that said plainly, "No smoking inside the house, thank you." He smiled at the thought, his head already smoky from the dope he and Ramona had smoked during the course of an afternoon of strong sexing.

"Phil, I don't know what you're making out of me . . . God! I just feel so horny all the time."

"Dr. Johnson, this is Phillip Dobson."

Elijah spilled a little of his duck turning to face Ramona and a bulldog of a brown-skinned man who had eased up to his left side. "Phillip, this is Dr. Mordecai Johnson . . ."

"I own the establishment," Dr. Johnson said metallically, dark circles rimming his eyes, shaking hands with Elijah as though he were handling a cold fish, all the while maintaining a constant vigilance over the gathering as he did so.

Motherfucker looks worried shitless, Elijah thought, watching the doctor's eyes shift from one person to another. He's watching people's hands, Elijah noted with surprise . . . watching people's hands to see that they don't steal something. Ain't that a bitch!

"What do you do, Mr. Dobson?" the doctor asked in a hard, flat voice, his eyes taking in everything.

"I'm an orgasm maker," Elijah cracked, testing the good doctor for some sign of life.

"Did I hear you correctly?" the doctor asked in the same hard, flat voice.

Elijah placed a hip, conciliatory-type smile between them, like, after all, we *are* soul brothers.

"Awwwww, I was just jokin', mannnn . . . I . . . uhh . . ." The doctor looked, glared into Elijah's face for the first time, contemptuously, and abruptly performed an about-face and waddled away.

Ramona leaned closer, her arms folded across her bosom, a frozen smile on her face, and whispered, "You didn't have to say that!"

"Fuck you talkin' 'bout, woman! didn't have to say what?!" Elijah raised his voice slightly, pissed off by the doctor's treatment, the general atmosphere, and now, by Ramona. Several people nearby turned to check them out.

"Phillip, you don't have to get all excited," she grated out between her teeth, trying to maintain. "All I said was . . ."

"Rahhhh mona!" two debutante types trilled in unison from halfway across the room and swayed over, all fashion and facade.

"Girrrrl! where in the world have you been keepin' yourself? I haven't seen you since the Morgan party."

"I haven't seen her since the Debs had their affair . . . I hear you're planning to get married? Reeelly!"

Elijah watched the three women stick their heads together right in front of him, looking, for all the world, like three teenagers talking on the telephone at the same time. Dizzy ass young bitches! don't really hardly know their asses from a hole in the ground. Parties, shopping, keeping up appearances for appearances' sake, doing what was supposed to be hip. He had to stop himself from sneering as they practically drug each other away by the armpits. Where were they going? To meet someone? take a triple-deck shit? smoke some opium in a far corner? ooopps, no smoking in the house. "Be right back, Phil . . . don't get lost," Ramona sang out super-sweetly as she was being pulled away. Elijah waved her away casually. They had saved her ass from a frightful chewing. The nerve of this young booshiee black bitch trying to tell me how to act! He snatched a fresh glass of something from a nearby buffet and wandered around the house feeling mean 'n evil. Big house. Rich. Shit hanging all over the walls. Phony ass people. He stood off to one side of the huge main room and shot out a host of bad vibes and one low-keyed fart toward an assembly of Ebony Fashion Show types grouped around the circular fireplace in the center of the room. Jiveass black motherfuckers! can't even talk right. Sound like they all got dictionaries in they mouths.

Her eyes met his from the other side of the fireplace and held. Once, twice, three times. Yeahhh, uhh huh, I'm for real, they seemed to say.

He looked around coolly, cautiously. Where is Ramona? What the hell, he decided, I shouldn't even be here with her square ass anyway.

He took his time circling to her side, checking for obstacles as he made his way.

He paused within her peripheral vision for a few minutes, giving her a full understanding of his intentions with his slow movements. Finally, he wedged himself next to her. "How you doin', Miss Lady?" he whispered near her ear.

She gazed up at him from her seat on the bricks, a nice even expression in her eyes. "Fine and you?" she answered in a low, private voice.

Elijah shrugged expressively. What could you say? He measured her three quarters of profile carefully. Thirty-one -two, maybe. Some kind of Indian woman, dress wrapped all 'round her body, close-cropped pixie haircut, bamboo cane earrings dangling. Pretty cocoa-colored lady, hip, Out There.

She gave his shrug a half smile and slowly returned her attention to the debate, showing obvious boredom with the proceedings.

He leaned back to her ear, a fine, delicate perfume floating up to his nose. "Uh, I notice you don't have a drink, can I get you one?" She turned her face fully to his.

"I'd rather have a smoke."

He juggled his cigarette pack out before realizing his mistake. A smoke?! a smoke . . . right on!

"Sorry 'bout that," he covered up suavely. "I got some smokes . . . but, uhhh . . ."

She stood up to reveal a well-designed five feet five. "Well, make a move, brother, I'm right behind you, ain't that the way it's supposed to be?"

The question sounded so sarcastic that he frowned.

"Well, *ain't* that the way it's supposed to be?" she repeated.

Elijah turned away without attempting an answer and walked ahead, clearing people from their path.

They were in the middle of the block when Elijah heard Ramona call him. "Phillip! Phillip! Phillip!"

He ignored the desperate voice, confident that she would never be indiscreet or indignant enough to come out onto the sidewalk.

He lit one of the joints, took a couple deep hits and passed it to her.

Toni Mathews clicked the radio onto the local jazz station.

"Did I hear your li'l ladyfriend call you Phillip?"

Elijah exhaled slowly, trying to look innocent.

She laughed softly in the darkness. "Awwww, c'mon on, you don't have to bullshit me. You should be able to tell by now that I'm regular people."

Elijah forced himself to laugh in turn. "My fo' real friends call me Elijah, Elijah Brookes. You didn't tell me your name?"

She sucked in a big swallow of smoke before replying. "I've been called a sack load of things, but *my* fo' real friends call me Toni, Toni Mathews."

"That's a pretty hip name," Elijah tried flattering her.

She shrugged and passed the joint back, three-fourths smoked. He pulled on it, down to the roach level, flicked it out of the window and lit another one.

They passed it back and forth, getting high.

"That's pretty mellow smoke," she announced after a few more hits.

"Glad you like it," he replied suavely, and slid down in the seat to let his mind play with the reflections on the water, the good herb smoke in his head, Mark on the radio, Toni's perfume, Toni Mathews.

He quietly turned to stare at her profile, suddenly loving the idea of being parked on the lakefront at half past midnight with an elegant, groovy sister.

"Can you dig this?" he asked, not indicating anything in particular, but everything . . .

"Uhh huh," she nodded, completely at ease, her head laid back on the seat, her eyes half slitted from the dope.

161

A few minutes later, minutes passing like giant globs of time, mistaking her quiet for an invitation, Elijah slid his right hand up the crease in the center of her dress, from knees to upper thighs.

"Oooh no, no baby." She eased his hand away gently. "No hot 'n heavy touchin'. Momma is on her bad days."

Elijah dealt with the putdown by sliding over against the door. Where is this bitch comin' from?

He felt like pressing the issue, but decided not to, for fear of being guilty of the kind of behavior that would cool out any future play, if there was going to be any . . . but, he was still feeling severely pissed. Where is this bitch comin' from?

After reordering himself, staring at the waves for a few minutes, he asked, in as cool a voice as he could manage, "Where would you like to go?"

Toni sighed, a little disappointed that he hadn't tried harder, but at the same time relieved because he hadn't.

By the time he made his way back to the block, driving as slowly as he could, he had decided that he definitely wanted to get next to her, in the worst way possible. There was something about her that turned him on. She was no Dee Dee, no Leelah, nor anything like the amateurs he had been playing on. She was a style of her own. An original.

"Uhhh, would it be possible to get in touch with you?" he asked, getting out of the car, hating himself for the tone of voice he heard creep into his question.

"Are you sure you want to?"

"Why not? shit, between the two of us, ain't no tellin' what we might get off into. I'm damned sure we can have a better time than we had tonight."

Toni looked up at him from the driver's seat and pouted her lips out at him playfully. "Awwww, did Momma give you a bad time, baby? here, let me kiss the bad vibes away."

She reached out for both sides of his face with her long-nailed fingers and spooled a half yard of lascivious tongue into his mouth.

He stood back to look at her after the kiss, trying to decide whether he should press his luck or control his frustration, or what?

Toni dug into her purse and handed him a card. "Don't call before six p.m., I don't get up 'til late, usually."

He solemnly saluted her with the card between his fingers as she pulled away, waving at him in her rear-view mirror. Wowwwww . . .

He strolled to his car, muted party sounds coming to him from down the street, Ramona Brown all but forgotten, sat at the curb thinking about the past forty-five minutes.

Miss Toni Mathews was obviously into something. He pulled the last joint out, the one he had been saving for the Total Experience Motel, lit it smiling at the memory, and wheeled away from the curb, the seeds of a game crinkling up his forehead . . . it would take some heavy sugar to get into a bitch like Toni, some heavy sugar.

CHAPTER 9

Elijah slouched inconspicuously at one of the stand-up desks alongside the east wall of the First National Bank, making all the motions to give the appearance of writing out a deposit or withdrawal slip, one eye on the plainclothes security man and the other one riveted on the slow actions of an apple-cheeked, blue rinse-haired grandmother type transacting business at a nearby window. He slowly, studiously scrawled a number of doodles on the withdrawal pad, allowing the grandmother maximum time to finish her drawn-out transaction and leave the bank before he followed. This was the eighth likely prospect he had tried to pin in three days. Was she with someone? Was she driving? Was she . . . ?! Beautiful!

From midway the block, he watched her stop in the southbound bus zone and casually check out the sign telling which busses were going where. Beautiful! the bus. What could be better?

He rushed to board the bus at the last minute, being very careful to keep himself fully out of the woman's sight.

He positioned himself close enough to observe her as they held onto the strap holders of the swaying, lurching bus. Sixty, if she's a day, not rich or else she wouldn't be on the bus, but not poor either, from the look of her garments. And kindly looking . . . yeahhh, kindly looking.

Yeahhh, this looked like the one, awright. There had only been one other one who seemed a more likely prospect before this one, but for some reason his instincts pulled him back from her. Something a li'l bit too robust about her, a li'l too keen looking. His heart thumped a little faster as the bus wound around a corner and headed into a Hyde Park route.

At this point, I wouldn't care if she was the chief of police's momma, I'd still make my play. A salt 'n pepper neighborhood to play in, not too much danger of someone calling the pigs just because a black had been spotted on the block. What could be better?

The game had buzzed around in his mind for a week after the party. When was that bitch going to answer her own telephone? "Don't call before six p.m., I don't get up 'til late, usually."

He reviewed the times he had called and left messages with her service. "Elijah, alias Phillip, called you six-fifteen." "Elijah Brookes, the First, called . . . seven-fifteen."

The corners of his mouth dragged down with the thought of his frustration. It never failed, let some cold-blooded bitch stick her finger up . . . oops . . . !

He shut off his other flow of thoughts and got back on his game; the grandmother was getting off the bus. The Hyde Park shopping plaza.

Rushing to get off, he almost knocked a middle-aged black woman with a shopping bag off her feet. She glared at him. "I swear fo' God, y'all . . ."

He was off the bus and trailing his prey at a discreet distance before the woman had finished her lecture on his manners. Be cool . . . be cool . . . he warned himself, filtering into the late-afternoon crowd of shoppers, strollers, Hare Krishna-ites, bearded University types, blacks, whites, Sikhs, yellows, the University of Chicago announcing itself through the interracial character of the neighborhood.

He followed her to the co-op supermarket and decided to wait in the mall . . . no need to follow the old girl around a damned supermarket, that would be, how would they say it? "counterproductive." He lounged around the front of the bookstore opposite the supermarket for a full ten minutes, studying titles and hairy-faced authors, wandered over into the big concrete patio of the mall and sat on a bench, waiting, a good profile of the supermarket's exit doors in view.

Assuring himself that he had the best seat in the house, to keep tabs on the lady, he gazed around the patio. A couple third-rate fiddlers scraping their hearts out about something. He gave them a half nod and a cold smile . . . they didn't seem to have too bad a hustle, if you had the patience to wait for enough suckers to fill up your hat.

A trio of white dudes with their hiking shoes laced

By Odie Hawkins

across their sleeping bag-back packs, full beards framing their innocent, sunburnt faces, limped past him, almost made him laugh aloud. The Eternal White Boy, never satisfied with life as it is, always got to try and make it harder. Too bad they couldn't've been born with some cold ashes in they jibbs.

Couple brothers with Japanese chicks . . . or Chinese, or whatever they were, hard to tell the difference . . . hmmm . . . that's a different scene. Niggers and chinks . . . yeahhh, that's sho' 'nuff a different scene.

A couple young sisters, skulls braided to the bone, swept through and gave him an opaque look. He gave them his full admiration look and received an even more opaque look in return. He crinkled the corners of his mouth into a sign of mild displeasure. Some of the latter-day sisters could be so stuck up 'n shitty sometimes. They talk about you like you stole something if you don't pay 'em no attention, and then, when you do, they look at you like you got a tail.

Damn! why won't this bitch give me a play? I guess I'll give her a ring later on, see what's happenin' . . .

He slouched on the bench and dug his hands deeper into his pockets. Got to leave the goddamned hosses alone, oats 'n blankets, that's all I'm doin' . . . buyin' oats 'n blankets for hosses. Gotta make a payment to Browney this weekend too. Wonder what Leelah is up to?

The sudden stress of all his things-to-do coming to his mind all at once almost made him miss the little grandmother, moving through the exit doors with a phalanx of evening shoppers.

Elijah stood and stretched himself indulgently. This is

167

it. He reviewed his list of needs and wants, used them to re-inforce his strategy . . . I needs this break, he whispered to himself.

He followed the woman, shopping bag in her left hand with a stalk of celery sticking out of it, wishing that he had all the answers to the questions he wanted to ask be-fore he really got off on her, but there was no way . . . he'd just have to play it by ear.

He bridged the distance between them, half running, when she turned into a four-storied courtway apartment. Damn it! don't tell me I'm gon' get this far and lose!

He peeked around the corner of the building at her back, checking her mailbox. He took in a couple deep breaths. Good thing old people move so slow. He gave her ten full minutes, from mailbox to apartment, walking slowly to the corner and back, before checking the name on the mailbox. Mrs. H.T. Campbell. Mrs.? No Mr.?

He pushed the buzzer under her name, adrenalin flowing moderately fast, prepared to deal with whatever. Campbell? What kind of name is that? Irish? . . . Scotch?

"Yessss?" A slightly hesitant voice came down through the intercom system.

"Don Adams, Mrs. Campbell, investigation unit of the First National Bank," he answered in his best blustering, authoritative voice. He smiled at the sudden buzz-in he re-ceived. People really nutted out behind official-sounding voices.

He deliberately slowed himself down on the way to the second floor; better to let her watch me approach than to open the door and get shook up by seeing my black ass in the doorway.

"Yessss?" Mrs. Campbell leaned out of her apartment, immediate apprehension forcing her left hand up to her throat at the sight of Elijah's dark, smiling face.

He whipped his phony I.D. card out, the one with his picture on it, as he approached the last three steps . . . best put the ol' girl as much at ease as possible.

"Good afternoon, Mrs. Campbell, my name is Donald Adams, investigation unit of the First National Bank. May I come in, please? I won't take more than a few minutes of your time."

He was easing past her into the apartment before she gave her consent, timing it to appear that he was accepting her invitation.

The first part was over . . . not too hard, people went for I.D. cards, especially white folks. He had noticed very early in his life of games . . . the proper I.D. card could work miracles.

"Yes . . . uhhh, come in." Mrs. Campbell slowly closed the door and stood with her hands clenched together at waist level. After all, he *was* black. "What can I do for you, Mr. Atkins?"

Elijah took his time, pressing the weight of his authority on her, setting his own rhythm. "Adams," he corrected her. "Mrs. Campbell, beautiful place you have."

"Thank you." She tried not to show too much pleasure with his statement. Her fingers unclenched slightly.

"May I sit down? It's been a long day already."

Mrs. Campbell graciously fluttered her hand toward one of her stuffed chairs.

Elijah, in turn, smiled her into the chair opposite him, a stuffed ottoman between them, and pulled a small black notebook out of his breast pocket. "I know you're puzzled by this visit, Mrs. Campbell. I'll try to explain it as quickly and clearly as I can."

He cleared his throat and concentrated on his diction . . . it wouldn't do to be slurrin' no words. How would a brother workin' for the bank talk? Was there anybody else in the place?

"We have serious reason to believe that the teller with whom you transacted business today is an embezzler."

With whom? with who? fuck it! it's said now.

Mrs. Campbell's hand shot up to her mouth as though she had heard a juicy bit of gossip. "Really? are you certain?"

He leaned forward slightly, jutting his chin out, playing. "No, we aren't certain, but we have, as I said, serious reason to suspect him. That is why I'm payin' you this visit, to ask your help in our investigation."

The sudden, sizzling whistle made him jump. Mrs. Campbell released a maternal smile all over him.

"It's just the teapot, Mr. Askins . . . it always scares people, would you care for a cup? . . . or a can of beer? My husband always drank beer."

"The name is Adams, Mrs. Campbell," he corrected her again and half stood, superpolitely, as she made a spritely move to the kitchen. "A cup of tea sounds great. I would like the beer but, well, being on duty 'n all, you understand."

"Yes, of course, I understand," she replied and disappeared through the dining room door.

Was she going to call the police?

He lowered himself back into the chair, breathing in shallow pools. Was she going for it? Things seem to be taking too long, I'd better speed the pace up a bit. More businesslike. Whiter.

What had she said? "My husband always drank beer." She ain't got no husband. Nobody else seems to be on the scene. Hurry up! goddamn it!

He sprang out of the seat to help her with the tray of teacups and saucers. Tea? oh wowwww . . .

"One or two?"

One or two? what the . . . ?! oh!

"Uhhh, two please." He settled back in the chair, controlling the slight case of nerves he felt. Teacup and two lumps. Hah! One sip. Two sips. Now!

"Mmmmm . . . that really hits the spot, Mrs. Campbell . . . now then . . ."

"Yes, I love a good cup of tea after a busy day, my husband used to . . ."

"Uhhh, yes, now then, Mrs. Campbell, before I go on, I must ask you to give me your word that you won't tell anybody about our investigation?"

The little old lady's sparkling blue eyes lit up, obviously intrigued by intrigue. "Ohhh, cross my heart 'n hope to die, sir."

"Uhhh hah hah hah, that won't be necessary, Mrs. Campbell." Elijah carefully placed his cup and saucer on the tray before going on. "What we're asking you, and nine other depositors, to do is this . . ."

The telephone ringing caused him to clench his back teeth together.

"Excuse me, that must be Doris."

"Doris?"

"Yes, my daughter, she worries so about me."

"Remember, Mrs. Campbell," he reminded her urgently. "Don't say a word about . . ."

She nodded in agreement, picking up the telephone. "Hello . . . yes, I thought it would be you, dear . . . yes . . ."

Elijah groaned inwardly. Was it going well? badly? was it going at all? He strained to listen to the mother-daughter dialogue. Why did she have to pick Now to call?

With nothing else to do for the ten minutes that Mrs. Campbell spent sighing, nodding, yessing, no-ing and giving advice, Elijah drank two more cups of tea.

Finally Mrs. Campbell hung up the phone and returned to her seat opposite him. "Doris wants to give me a couple kittens, she thinks I ought to have more living things in the house. I told her, my plants are . . ."

"Yes, they really are beautiful," Elijah interrupted suavely, glancing around at the small, potted jungle behind his chair. "Really beautiful. As I was saying, Mrs. Campbell . . ."

"Yes? yes? you were saying?"

Good. She's still right there.

"The First National Bank is asking you and nine other depositors for help in capturing an embezzler."

"My help? what can I . . . ?"

"Here is what we want you to do . . . I hate to rush through this, Mrs. Campbell, but I have three other depositors to see this evening. We want you—" He took a slight pause for emphasis, "to withdraw half your savings."

He paused again, this time to study the little old lady's reaction. It was positive. She was nodding amiably, waiting for instructions.

"We don't really care how much you withdraw, as long as it's half. Oh, before I go on, did I mention that you and the other cooperating depositors would receive bonus interest rates for the next six quarters, as well as a modest reward?"

Mrs. Campbell, taken in by Elijah's earnest, sincere manner, practically thanked him. "The First National wants me to withdraw half my savings? That would be . . ."

He waved her to a stop. "Please, Mrs. Campbell, the amount doesn't matter to me . . . the accounting section will deal with that. We'd simply like to have your withdrawal tomorrow morning, say, between eleven and twelve o'clock? Your savings will then be re-deposited, the accounting section will double-check the master accounting ledgers and, hopefully, we'll be able to find out who is stealin' our money . . . hah hah hah."

Mrs. Campbell nodded in agreement as Elijah stood up to leave, totally involved with the idea of justice being done.

"I'd like to remind you," he cautioned her, "this is a top secret operation."

He paused to purse his mouth, pantomiming a zip the lips gesture. "I'll return tomorrow afternoon at exactly two o'clock, re-deposit your funds and . . . well, what can I say, Mrs. Campbell? Thank you for your cooperation."

"I'm glad to be able to offer my cooperation, Mr. Adams . . . the nerve of that rascal!" Mrs. Campbell stated flatly, and stuck her hand out, good buddy-old pal fashion.

He shook her hand warmly, lit his face up with just the right amount of smile, officialdom being human.

"Oh, one other thing, Mrs. Campbell, our investigation will be completed by the end of this month and there's bound to be some publicity, a newspaper article, at least. You wouldn't be too put out by havin' your picture in the news, would you? maybe a television interview?"

"Ohhh, no, not at all." Mrs. Campbell beamed at the possibility.

"Well then, until tomorrow, Mrs. Campbell . . . take care, thank you for the tea. Remember, between eleven and twelve? We have other people scheduled for the hours before and after that time.

She flashed him the round, doughnut A-okay sign and winked.

Elijah floated down the stairs. How lucky could you be? Am I really over? was she really in the bag? or was she calling her daughter and every goddamned body within dialing distance, to blab about this secret bank thing she was involved with?

Well, the proof of the pudding would be in the eating . . . and that wouldn't take place until tomorrow.

He raced to catch a bus back downtown, to retrieve his car, mentally slashing back and forth across his game. Did I lay it on too thick? Did I lay it on thick enough?

Lemme see, today is Wednesday. She gets the dough out tomorrow, I give her a receipt . . . that's Thursday. She wouldn't, shouldn't begin to get suspicious before Friday, maybe Monday.

He plunked himself down into a seat by the window,

brooding and gloating with the idea of the possibility of success. How much did she have in the bank? Ten grand? Twenty? Wowwww . . . what if the old bitch had a million dollars?! The thought stunned his mouth open for a split second. Nawwwww, ain't nobody got a million dollars. Awww shit! why didn't I offer to take her to the bank and pick her up!? Damn!

Elijah nodded congenially to the early evening regulars in the Afro Lounge, headed straight for the telephone hung midway between the mens and womens, his nose smarting from a couple thick lines of recently snorted girl.

He banged the telephone back into the receiver the minute the message unit started. Bitch! What the fuck was she trying to pull off?!

He held her card up and glared at it for the umpteenth time. Toni Mathews, it said, and her telephone number and that was all. He slipped the card back into his wallet and strolled out to the bar, feeling a little confused and sorry for himself, despite the nervous energy released in him by the cocaine.

"What'll it be?" the lady bartender, in tune with all the latest twists and turns of fortune, fixed her brightest smile on him.

"Lemme have a double Bristol Cream," he growled, dark, evil thoughts on his mind.

The bartender's smile lapsed into a coma . . . niggers could be so unpredictable sometimes.

"What's goin' on, man? you look like your dick won't ever get hard again." Elijah looked up from his second double Bristol Cream. Good ol' Sid, you could always count on him to say something outrageous, with his sausage pouch eyes.

"What's to it, Sid? Buy you a taste?"

Sid mounted the stool next to Elijah, being careful to pull his creases tight so that his pants wouldn't get baggy at the knees. "Yeah, I could dig some kind of refreshment. Lemme have a shot o' that Regal, willya, babysweets?"

The two men sat next to each other for a full minute, sipping their drinks, unhurried by life, into games and scenes, fraternity brothers.

"Couple dagos was through here a li'l while ago, askin' 'bout you," Sid opened up casually.

"Oh yeah? you know 'em?" Elijah asked, trying to be equally casual.

Sid grimaced behind a swallow of his drink and signalled silently for the bartender to give him a glass of water. "Nawww, not really, I know their types though. You got a bad scene goin' on somewhere?"

Elijah felt the sudden urge to tell Sid to mind his own business, but then realized that he was dealing with one of his main men, someone who had always been on the good side of Righteous with him. "Uhhh, nawww, you know how it is."

"Yeahhh, yeah, I'm hip to it." Sid nodded, reading between the lines of the verbal shorthand, "But you best git yo' shit together, them dagos don't be jivin', man."

Elijah slapped Sid's outstretched hand lightly, in affirmation. "Yeah, I hear ya, blood, I hear ya ... everything gon' be extremely cool by this time next week, extremely cool . . . I got a thang in the works right now."

Did the old broad call her daughter and blab? Are the pigs goin' to be waitin' for my black ass tomorrow? Why didn't I offer the old bitch a ride to the bank? Damn! that would've really tightened it all up.

Now Browney is on my case. Shit!

Sid carefully drained his glass and slowly dismounted, as much concern as could possibly be shown on his poker face. "Take care, bruh . . . you know how cold-blooded them motherfuckers is."

"Right on! right on!" Elijah bluffed off the solemn warning, unusual, coming from cynical Sid. "Take care yourself, man."

"I'm gon' do that," Sid said quietly, and eased off to the Stickhall in search of fresh blood.

Elijah screwed his glass around in the water print it had made. Yeahhh, I must needs take care that business . . . how much am I in the hole now?

"Can I get you another drink? ahhhem . . . ?"

"Huh? . . . oh?"

"I said, can I get you another drink?"

Another drink? Yeah, why not? nothing else to do 'til two p.m. tomorrow. "Yeah, baby . . . gon' do it again."

The bartender lady refilled Elijah's glass, looking up as quickly as he did when two neighborhood regulars popped in. It paid to be on your ps 'n qs at all times, no tellin' when someone was going to pop in the door and throw a knife, a brick, a bottle or just simply shoot.

Elijah sat, twirling the glass by the stem, feeling the urge to do ten things, and nothing, at the same time. Wonder if

I could rap to Browney? maybe cool him out 'til next week?

He smiled at his own bad, silent joke. You didn't rap to Browney, you didn't cool him out. You paid him. Period. Interest on the principle, and more interest, all the time. God! I hope this ol' bitch has a hundred grand.

He stood up suddenly, the thought of Toni Mathews being at home wisping through his subconscious, and just as suddenly reseated himself. Fuck her! wait 'til I get my pockets stuffed with grand-theft dough.

He turned to look around at the people scattered around the lounge. Typical Wednesday night group. Nine-thirty. Too early for the heavyweights. He winked at the two middle-aged sisters in lavender, rose and hot pink, but decided to be cool.

Wonder if li'l Miss Brown got married yet? Wonder if li'l Miss Brown got home from the party yet? I can just see her now, trying to look up Phillip Dobson in the phone book . . . she and about ten other bitches. Clotille.

Clotille. The name triggered two separate thoughts in his head . . . Mabel Stewart from long ago. Last year? three years ago? and the sound of B.B. King's voice singing "The Thrill is Gone."

He turned around again to check out the lavender, rose and hot pink duo. It was obvious from the way that they were deliberately ignoring him that they were interested.

Nawww, I'd best keep my energy together for tomorrow. Just wait 'til I get a chance to rap to Toni . . . I'm gon' blow that bitch's ear off!

"How much I owe you, doll?" The bartender lady moved quickly to the space in front of Elijah, doing abacus calculations as he moved. Wonder if I could pad it for a dollar 'n a quarter? he looks fucked up. Might not remember whether or not his partner had a double or a single . . .

"That'll . . . be ten dollars even."

Elijah gave her a nasty, sneering smile and announced in a loud, loud voice, "My tab is eight dollars and seventy-five cents. I had three double Bristols at two fifty a glass and my man had a single shot of Chivas Regal at a dollar 'n a quarter. That comes to eight seventy-five! What the fuck you tryin' to do, cheat me!?"

The bartender lady allowed herself to be humbled by Elijah's tirade. After all, the customer *was* always right. "Sorry, I made a mistake," she mumbled softly, dropping her eyes slightly, paying dues.

"You motherfuckin' right! you made a mistake!" Elijah played the irate customer all the way home and slammed a twenty down onto the bar.

After she had carefully counted his change out in front of him, half the people in the bar looking on with jaded indulgence, he slid two dollars back across the bar and leaned across to whisper, "Remember, baby . . . you can't cheat an honest man."

Elijah carefully recounted the money on the dining room table, keeping his voice to a steady monotone as he came to the final figure again. Two thousand, five hundred dollars.

"That's it, Mrs. Campbell," he announced in a dry, official tone, "two thousand, five hundred dollars."

Mrs. Campbell stood with her arms folded across her

lank breasts, a vague expression on her face. "That's a lot of money, isn't it? Mr. Adams . . . I don't think I've ever seen quite so much money at once."

Elijah's eyes traveled quickly over the short, green stacks of fifty-dollar bills. Damn! only twenty-five hundred! damn!

"We see that much, and a whole lot more, every day, down at the bank, Mrs. Campbell."

"Ohhh, yes, I'll bet you do! I'll bet you do." She brightened up slightly as she spoke, thinking of her role in the solution of a crime.

Elijah forced himself to calmly pull out his carefully designed receipt book, an expensive creation by a thug buddy who had majored in printing in Statesville. He scribbled twenty-five hundred, Mrs. H.T. Campbell, dated the receipt and with a flourish, signed, "Donald T. Adams, special investigator, Security Division, First National Bank."

"Here you are, Mrs. Campbell." He handed her the receipt, opened his small attache case, a relic from his pots 'n pans day, carefully arranged the money inside, clicked it closed and reached to shake Mrs. Campbell's hand.

He had toyed with the idea of using a diplomatic courier's wrist chain, doing a superdramatic bit of clicking the bracelet on his wrist and locking the other end to the attache case, but decided against it because it might seem too corny.

Mrs. Campbell squeezed his hand tightly with both of hers. "My . . . uhhh . . . everything will be all right, won't it, Mr. Adams? I mean . . ."

He fixed a kind, gentle, warm expression on his face and reassured her. "Your money is absolutely safe with First National, Mrs. Campbell, please be assured of that . . . your receipt is a double safeguard."

He moved quickly to the door, hating the pitiful, trusting puppy dog look in her eyes. "Once again, Mrs. Campbell, thank you for your cooperation . . . I'm sure you'll be very pleased with your bonus interest rates and, I'm not supposed to tell you this . . ." He opened the door and peeked out theatrically. "Your reward will be two hundred and fifty cash dollars."

Mrs. Campbell clasped her hands together in delighted surprise, looking, with the gesture, like a TV giveaway prize winner. "Oooooohhhhh!"

Elijah felt a trickle of sweat run down his side. God! the door is open, I'm on my way. "Goodbye, Mrs. Campbell, see you in the newspaper," he said, and took a step out of the door.

"Oh, Mr. Adams, won't you need my bankbook?"

It seemed, for a moment, that time was suspended and that Mrs. Campbell's right hand was floating into her apron pocket and pulling out her bankbook in slow motion. The whole thing! she was giving him the whole thing!

He stared at the little blue book and did some electronic thinking. The bankbook? Today is Thursday, nobody around that I trust at the moment . . . by Friday, anybody walking in for the other half might get hassled and busted, leading to me . . . and by Monday it would definitely be unsafe.

He took a step back into the apartment. "No, Mrs. Campbell, your bankbook won't be necessary. I thought I explained . . . I will re-deposit your money, or Mrs. MacElroy, one of our administrative assistants, will . . . and it will be automatically credited to your account by way of our computer coding process."

Mrs. Campbell shook her head in wonder at all the marvelous, sophisticated ways of the world and pushed her bankbook back down into her pocket. "You people think of everything, don't you, Mr. Adams?"

"We try to, m'am." Elijah smiled easily and waved as he started down the stairs. Home free! if the F.B.I. wasn't waiting in front of the apartment. Home free!

He squared his shoulders and marched out of the courtway, knowing that Mrs. Campbell was digging him from her front window. He turned the corner of the apartment building and felt like running to his car, but decided to be cool and walk . . . it would never do, to twist an ankle or something, with two and a half grand to be spent . . . never.

CHAPTER 10

Elijah sprawled out in his favorite easy chair, music on his box, a stick of high-grade grass in the corner of his mouth, slowly roving his eyes around his new apartment. Furnished with all the necessities, ultra delooxe, two hundred and seventy-five a month.

He sucked a bit of smoke into his lungs. Two hundred and seventy-five bucks per month, plus all the other b.s., but it was boss. Yeahhh, outta sight. But this is the way I been wanting it for a long time. Pockets pumped full of stolen coin, a groovy crib, a nice ride, what else do I need?

Without giving it very much serious thought, he reached over and dialed Toni Mathews' number, the exchange memorized now. After four rings he was about to hang up, to forget all about it, when Toni's voice came through, heavy from sleep.

"Helloooooooo?" She stifled a giant yawn. All of his re-hearsed rhetoric, all of the violent language he had planned to release in her ear, whenever he caught her on the phone, skidded out into left field. He settled back in his chair to rap, opened up with as mellow a tone as his voice could manage. "Heyyyy there, Miss Lady . . . this is brother Elijah."

"Who?" she asked.

His body stiffened slightly. She had to be jivin' . . . be-hind all the messages he had left.

"Me, baby . . . *Mr.* Elijah Brookes, the First," he answered coldly, falling back slightly into his groove.

"Ooooohhh, hi ya doin', luv?" she responded warmly, all trace of sleep and b.s. gone from her voice. "Say, look, I know you've been tryin' to reach me . . ."

"For weeks, almost."

"Yeah, I can dig it; I've just been so tied up with one thing and another. Look, could I ask you to please call me back a li'l later? Say, a couple hours from now? I've got some business that I absolutely must take care of, within the next half-hour, if I don't, my name will be mud junior."

Elijah took a deep hit on the joint, his head throbbing suddenly with a frustrated headache. "Yeah, I can do that. Are you definitely sure you want me to?"

For a few seconds it seemed that her connection had died in his ear, or that she had covered up the receiver. "You know I do," she finally answered, her voice firm and honest.

"Awright, later then."

He slowly replaced the receiver, feeling elated and depressed at the same time. What is it the old people used to say? . . . "the melon that you've waited the longest to steal usually tastes the sweetest."

He laid his head back on the headrest and pulled hard on the joint. Was she worth it? Up to this point he had been so involved with the pursuit part that he had never really considered any other section. Is she worth it?

He blew a small jet stream of smoke up to the ceiling, floating into the lived-in voice of Billie Holiday singing "Sophisticated Lady."

The softly clanging chimes startled him. Who could it be? Only three people, aside from the telephone company, knew where he lived.

He eased over to the fisheye peephole in the front door. Two white dudes. Who could they be? and how could they have gotten in without buzzing? And they told me that this fuckin' place was well-guarded.

One of the dudes rang again. And again. And again. Elijah felt paranoia creeping up the back of his skull. Pigs? Yeah! pigs!

He raced away from the front door, snatched his wallet from the dresser, grabbed his leather jacket from the closet and made tracks to the back door.

Damn!

He stopped dead in front of the back door, his hand reaching out for the knob. If it was the pigs, they probably had twice times the number of people at the back door as they had at the front. He flung his jacket down on the kitchen table in disgust, tears swelling up in his eyes. Goddamn it to hell!

He shuffled back through the apartment, the chimes clanging in his ears like doom bells, arrogantly lit a half-smoked joint and strolled to the door. What the fuck! why not go out with style?

"Yeah! who could it be?" he asked sarcastically.

"Police!" a bass voice rumbled back at him.

He opened the door and graciously waved the two swarthy, tallish, well-built men into the apartment, insolently blowing smoke into their faces as they passed by him.

"Uhh, may I see some I.D., officers? Do y'all have a search warrant? Are you sure you're in the right place? Lots o' mistakes been happenin' these days, you know?"

The shortest of the two, the six-footer, playfully punched Elijah on the shoulder.

"Relax, relax, Elijah. We ain't the cops." The other man strolled in, looking around carefully, sat in Elijah's easy chair, pulled out a German luger and laid it in his lap, his face a mask.

Without asking, he knew who they were now. His shoulders slumped a little. Were they going to throw him out of the window? the way they had done Duke "Dice" Manson, a few years back? or break his thumbs, the way they had done the Jewish call girl a few weeks ago? The newspapers had printed a lot of bullshit, all of the In people knew what had gone down.

Or were they just going to kill him?

"What can I do for you guys?" he asked in a shaky voice, measuring the distance he'd have to cover to the door, dodging luger shells.

The luger man reached into his inside breast pocket and

186

passed his partner a sheet of paper.

The man standing in front of him spoke with a cold smile on his lips. "Browney, your friend, sent us over to remind you that you owe him, as of today, exactly one thousand, two hundred bucks and ten cents interest, plus two hundred bucks. You wanna pay all or part of it now?"

Elijah looked at him as though he were speaking a lost language. "How much?" He finally worked the question out.

"One thousand, two hundred and ten cents plus two hundred. Which comes to one thousand, four hundred 'n ten cents. You hard o' hearin'?"

The luger man's face creased in an animal grimace that was meant to be mistaken for a smile.

Elijah's shoulders slumped a little more.

"Uhh, nawww, hah hah hah . . . I, uhhh . . . I just hadn't realized it was that much."

"That's how much it is," the man in the chair spoke for the first time. "How much do you wanna give us? the whole pie or just a piece?"

Elijah could feel the nervous tic creep up his cheek and felt powerless to prevent it. "Dig, fellas . . . I'm a li'l low right in through here, I got a deal that's about to go down."

"How much, man?" the luger man cut in.

"Well, I can give you a couple bills now . . . and then, when my . . . uhhh . . . deal comes through . . ."

"Fuck the con, Elijah, we want the dough."

Elijah dug down into his wallet and pulled out four fifties from the rest of the bills in the wallet.

The man in the easy chair slid out of it, his piece in Elijah's face, as his partner snatched his wallet out of his hands and pulled the rest of the bills from it. He fanned the bills out like cards, three hundred dollars' worth, divided the money with his partner and said, "That's it, huh? two hundred on your account."

"Not unless you gon' add that other three!?" Elijah shot in, his anger at being robbed overcoming his fear.

Both of the men laughed. "Nawww, we don't include that. Let's just call that a gift from you to us."

"A gift?!"

"Yeah," the luger man added, "a gift for not breakin' your fuckin' head."

Elijah looked down slightly, not wanting to give any provocation at this point.

The two men moved, in step, to the door. "We don't make but two visits, Elijah . . . remember that." The taller of the two held up one finger to indicate that they had made one already, and slammed out.

Elijah stood in the center of the room, shaking with fear and rage. Dirty, rotten, cold-blooded motherfuckers! Dirty rotten . . .

He stumbled to his chair, feeling wasted. Son-bitches! opened his wallet to stare at the empty space left by the removal of his money. Oh well, I guess if you play with the bull you got to get a li'l horn sometimes.

Feeling a bit steadier after a few minutes of serious thinking, he eased into his bedroom and lifted the mattress . . . six hundred dollars' worth of fifty-dollar bills stared back at him.

How much have I paid that leech? Seven, eight hundred

bucks? and it still goes on. How much did the muscle say I owed? A grand-four hundred.

He picked up two of the fifty-dollar bills and stuffed them into his pocket. One thousand and four hundred bucks . . . not really too much, really.

All I got to do is make another big score and I can pay the whole business off for good. The mistake I been makin', he rationalized, is tryin' to pay it off in bits 'n pieces.

Leaning closer to stare at his bloodshot eyes in his dresser mirror, he smiled cutely at his image. Things weren't really too bad . . . just a momentary scare, a minor hassle that could be squared away. Anything that could be squared away with money was a minor hassle, no more, no less.

Feeling braver, he grazed his right hand across his chin. Think I'll do myself a close shave and get out into these terrible streets, see what I can catch . . . I need a li'l relaxation.

Elijah stood at the long bar, a tall, fancy drink in front of him, squeaky clean, staring at Toni Mathews. Caesars. Yeah, Caesars *would* we the kind of place she'd go to . . . half-ass plush, filled to the brim with upper-crust slicksters.

He took a short sip of his drink, to wet his lips, stiffened his back as he made his way through the tables to her table.

He approached her at an oblique angle, just as she and the five other people stood up to leave. Three men and three women. Which one of the men was her man?

The angle of their exit placed him behind them . . . he moved a little quicker. Ain't no way I'm gon' let you get away.

He eased up behind her in the velveteen-draped foyer.

"Well, well . . . if it ain't Mizz Toni, herself."

She turned to him with a seductive curl to her mouth. "Hi you doin', Elijah . . . ! I saw you at the bar and I was goin' to come over to you but I could see that you were comin' to me. I thought you were goin' to call back this afternoon?"

Elijah cocked his head to one side. After all the times he had tried to reach her, and finally did, she would manage to snag him on a technicality. He noticed her friends moving a discreet distance away, evidently they were all just friends and nothing more. "Uhhh, well, somethin' came up that sort of tuned everything out, including the return call. Say, look, why don't we stop this Mickey Mouse bullshit . . . ?"

"Toni!?" one of the men called to her.

"Be right with you, Bob," she signalled to him.

"Tell me," Elijah rushed on, "either you have some time for me or you don't. Now which is it gon' be?"

She patted him on the cheek and he didn't know whether or not he dug it. "You're a pretty direct type dude, aren't you?"

"Gotta be, baby . . . life is too short for a bunch o' jive."

They stared into each other's eyes for a few hot seconds, a nice visual suggestion being created.

She dug down into her purse . . .

"Oh oh, here we go again," he cracked.

"Nope, not really," she said and scribbled her address on the back of one of her cards. "Look, I gotta run now. I'm havin' a few people over tomorrow night. Can you make it? We can sit off in a corner somewhere and rap."

Elijah gave the card an elaborately shaped kiss. "I'll be

there with bells on."

"Beautiful! see you," she sang out and glided away.

He watched her join her circle of people, joining and leading, he noticed. She sho' is a bad bitch. He stood rooted to the spot like a love-struck mark, smelling the subtle scent she had trailed behind her, her way of talking, the thing she had with her hands, her . . . her . . . her her-ness, he finally decided after struggling for a complete description of what she was in his eyes.

He became conscious of several dudes standing off to one side, checking him out with cynical, cold smiles on their faces. He pocketed the card and turned away abruptly . . . I better be cool, people'll be thinkin' that I got my nose open.

"Man can't never tell what he gon' do 'til he gets in that situation."

Elijah patiently mumbled, "Right on," to Home's soliloquy, his mind miles away. At any other time he might have dug the barber's constant, lightweight folktalking, but for now, he felt himself going up and down. Why couldn't he just go on and cut hair?

"And to top it off," Home swept grandly from one section of his spirit life to another, "would you b'lieve this chick comes to the door after I done sat out front on the steps, drinkin' moonshine 'n cryin' . . . she comes to the door and says, 'Home, whatchu doin' out here? why didn't you knock so I could let you in? You gonna catch yo' death o' cold, or get the piles sittin' out there! come on in, baby!'"

"What did you do, Home? kick her teeth down her throat?" Elijah asked, feeling obligated to snake some sort of moral comment.

"Nawww, nawww . . . if I'da lissened to my first mind, that's what I woulda done, but the minute she put them steamin' hot arms 'round my neck I just melted. And I ain't jivin' when I say I had actually felt my knees buckle when I passed the bedroom window and seen Joe Gales' ol' rusty black ass doin' the rooty tooty."

The customers sitting along the wall, waiting their turn, cracked up. The bursts of laughter jacked Elijah's spirits up a bit, taking his mind away from the blues.

"So, don't tell me what a man won't do, 'specially when it come to a woman."

Home flashed his big kidney-shaped mirror in front of Elijah's face for his approval.

Elijah carefully studied the contoured lines of his natural. No doubt about it, Home was a helluva barber, worth driving halfway across the city for.

"How you like it, home?"

"You on your job, Home . . . on your job," Elijah re-affirmed the barber's pride in his craft and tipped him a dollar.

"Awright, next man! ooooops! sorry 'bout that. Next brother, I forgot, we into a stone natural bag now."

"Right on, Home!" the customer, a two hundred and twenty-pound steel-workin' man, replied.

Elijah dipped over to the manicurist. "Pearl, I want you to do my nails up so good that folks'll be tryin' to reach out in the dark to sniff the tip ends."

Pearl, in tune, smiled sweetly and countered, "If they ain't already doin' that, baby . . . there ain't a manicure in the world that's gon' make it happen."

"Right on, sister woman," Elijah agreed and sat down opposite her without any other attempts at levity.

He felt a cold chill sweep up the back of his neck, despite the heat of the afternoon, as he spotted the car ease up behind him at the curb. The voice chilled him even more.

"Heyyy, 'Lijah baby . . . wha's happenin'?"

He turned slowly, feeling almost cold with mean vibes. Of all the people.

He inclined his upper body slightly, trying not to give away too much ground. Murphy and Jackson watched his movements closely.

"Good afternoon, Detective Murphy . . . Detective Jackson," he replied formally, trying not to look too closely at either one of them.

"Been hearin' brave things about you, brother . . . brave things." Jackson ignored his greeting for a dig.

"Get in, blood . . . let's cut up a few minutes."

Elijah straightened his back. "I'm in a hurry, that is, 'less y'all makin' me get in?"

The two detectives exchanged snide looks. Murphy appointed himself spokesman for the two. "Nawwww, ahhh nawwww, nothin' like that, 'Lijah. We just wanted to rap with you for a bit. No hard feelin's, huh?"

Elijah tried, but couldn't prevent himself from scowling. "Would it matter if I had hard feelin's?"

"Not really," Jackson snapped at him.

"If that's the case, then why don't we leave it that way?"

"Awright with me, brother. That okay with you, bruh' Murphy?"

"Yeahhh, fine with me. I don't give a damn if he don't wanna be my friend. But I tell you what, if you gon' be like that, make sure your shit is smellin' super good when it spills out."

He was afraid to let the curse out before they eased off down the street, afraid that they would really hassle him. Bastards! Thought somebody told me that they had been sent 'way out into the boondocks, for messing with somebody? Guess they must be using an off day to get in on some of this good ol' black Saturday night corruption 'n graft. Bastards!

He doubled his movement to the Afro Lounge, determined not to have anything foul up his preparations for the evening.

As usual, a few of the regulars sat at the tables in the back, champin' at the bit, waiting for Saturday night to really get on. Elijah slid onto a bar stool.

The lady bartender, recognizing Elijah's affluence, from rumor and fact, swiveled over to him. "What'll it be, Mr. Brookes?"

"You, baby, you," he responded automatically.

"I'm expensive, how about a drink?"

"Mix me somethin' strange 'n wonderful."

"How 'bout a Haitian voodoo?"

"That sounds groovy. Chink been through?" She checked her watch as though she were timing something.

"Not yet, should be comin' through in a few minutes. A few other people back there are waitin' on him too."

He sat, sipping his voodoo, watching the bartender tend bar, winking at her from time to time.

She came over to light his cigarette, in between customers. "You know somethin', Elijah . . . ?"

"What's that, baby?"

"If I thought you weren't just jivin', I might see my way clear to give you some of my time."

"If I thought you wasn't just jivin', I'd let you do that."

They exchanged understanding smiles. Players.

She hustled away to deal with a trio of afternoon stragglers. Chink made his entrance, a small, yellow, slit-eyed fox of a man . . . cynical smile on his thin lips.

"What's happenin', Elijah? us po' folks don't see too much of you these days."

"I'm in and out. How's the business?"

"Could be better. What can I do for you?"

Elijah pantomimed a television-headache commercial. "I could use something for this headache in my nose."

Chink looked disdainfully at the anxious collection of dope fiends at the rear of the bar. "Meet me in my office, soon as I take care of these brothers, okay?"

Elijah nodded and turned back to his drink, everything cool now, knowing that the Chink had taken his order and would deliver, the minute he got to the men's room. He nonchalantly checked out the rush-hour movement that developed behind Chink. For the umpteenth time he considered the dope trade, meaning heroin, how much it would take to get into it, how much you could get out of it, and rejected the idea once again. He felt no moral repulsion, no ill will toward the dealer, it just wasn't his stick.

He counted twelve anxious bodies going into the men's, and twelve anxious faces coming out.

He slipped off the stool and strolled to the back, no dope fiend, no anxiety about his movement.

Chink leaned against the rear wall of the toilet, his body tense, alert.

"How much?" he asked without preliminaries, all business with the business.

Elijah held out a fifty. Chink took it, looked at it closely, smiled his foxy little smile and spoke out of the barred window. "One spoon," he said.

A mysterious hand held up an aluminum foil after a few seconds. Chink took it and passed it to Elijah.

"How is it?" Elijah asked.

"The best," Chink answered, not one to play around with many words.

Elijah took a deep breath and eased out, he was ready now. The Chink really has a neat li'l setup, he thought, passing through the bar, home bound . . . all of the weight is on the man outside, if the narcs should bust in on him, he's clean.

Wonder who the mule outside the window is?

Elijah, a towel saronged around his waist, stroked his freshly shaven chin and stared down at the party garments he had laid out on the bed. It was the chartreuse three-piece pinstripe, with the French ruffles in the split on the bell-bottoms that caused him double thought. What kind of people are she gon' have at her set? He turned away from his sartorial dilemma to roll up a crisp fifty-dollar bill, leaned over his dresser to snort two more lines of the twelve he had laid out on its polished glass top.

Snuffling, he turned around and decided, the cocaine suffusing his nasal membranes, to wear the chartreuse. What the fuck do I care, anyway, about who's gon' be there? I'm gon' be there!

He sat on the side of his bed, a cold burn in his nostrils. Yeahhh, Chink said it was the best . . . wowwww . . .

Feeling powerful, he leaned back on his elbows and looked up at the ceiling.

How will I handle this bitch? so far it's been a Chinese standoff, with her almost winning. He reviewed possible methods of attack. Can't drive on her. I tried that.

He straightened up slowly. "Momma's on her bad days." I'll bet she was connin' me. Yeahhh, I'll bet she was connin' me.

Pulling his paisley jockey shorts up over a semi-troublesome erection, he flashed on a sexual conquest. Maybe I could fuck her into my corner. He patted the bulge in his shorts and rejected that approach. Fuckin' a bitch into your corner ain't too hip, the minute you decide that you too tired, or got too much else on your mind, or you just don't feel like it, everything goes right out the window.

He bent over gracefully to snort two more lines, loving the feel of silk and nylon on his body. Straightening up slowly from the coke, he stared at himself in the mirror.

Maybe I could make her fall in love with me? The image in the mirror frowned and seemed to ask, how do I do that?

He turned away from the frowning figure in the mirror after a full minute, certain that the answer to the question of how he could make Toni Mathews fall in love with him was to . . . fall in love with her.

He pulled on his pants, snuffling and snorting the dry phlegm down his throat, loving and hating the alkaloid aftertaste. Praise be to the Chink, who giveth us Almighty Coke!

Laughing aloud at the thought, he slid his arms into an off-lemon-colored shirt. Elijah Brookes, in love!? That sho' 'nuff is a laugh.

Buttoning his shirt up, he turned super serious. But do I love her? The weight of the thought pushed him down into a slumped, sitting position on the side of the bed.

Ain't this a bitch! I'm in love. In love with a bitch that I ain't never done nothin' with but kiss, and she was the one that did that. We ain't fucked, ain't had no kind o' dealin's at all, and I'm in love. What kind o' fucked-up trip is this?

Could Toni love me? Does she know as little about the whole thing as I do?

He whipped a beaver-tailed tie around his neck, took it off, wrapped it around again and finally decided to leave it off altogether. Niggers should never wear neckties, considerin' how many of our necks've been stretched.

He bent over to snort up the last two lines, his whole being cocaine light, his thoughts sweeping from place to place in supersonic fashion.

It's true, I don't know a goddamned thing about it, about what the squares call love.

He slurred the word disdainfully through his mind. Love . . . what the fuck was it, really?

I guess it's this, he said to himself in ultra-sober fashion, making final adjustments on himself in the mirror.

"Mirror, mirror on the wall, please don't tell all, but is not Elijah the fairest nigger of them all?"

Laughing at his own ego trip, he gently patted a palmful of Canoe on both cheeks and strode out of his apartment as though he were cake-walking past a brigade of inspecting generals.

CHAPTER 11

Despite the fact that there were at least fifty people making up the immediate background, he could see only one.

She leaned against the door frame, a cocoa-colored vision in a long, split up to the thighs skirt, capped by a brocaded bolero jacket, barely shielding a wisp of a bra.

He felt his eyes being pulled toward her by the ruby stuck in her navel. Wowwww . . . and I thought my chartreuse pinstripe was gon' be radical!

She stepped out of the door frame and greeted him with a kiss. "I didn't think you were comin'," she said quietly and led him into the apartment.

"You really know how to turn folks on and off, don't you?"

"I'm in no position to take chances with strays," she spoke in the same quiet voice.

Elijah bristled up slightly, the cocaine feeding him little jolts of ego. "If I look like a stray to you, you don't know a pedigreed nigger when you see one! what kinda jazz is this you be tryin' to pull . . . ?"

She linked her arm through his and tapped her forefinger across his lips. "No bad vibes tonight, okay? I feel too groovy for bad vibes."

He smiled sheepishly, cooled out, and let himself be guided through the crowd to one of the three bars positioned around the huge room.

"Is your man here?" he whispered to her as they approached the bar.

"My men are everywhere," she answered with an arrogant turn of her head. "What would you like?"

"I been hornin' coke all evenin', I'd hate to mess that up with anything else."

Without another word, she led him across the room, to the bar at the opposite side of the room, whispered into the bartender's ear, below the plush sounds of East Indian ragas and down-home blues. The bartender placed two miniature spoons of cocaine, styled like miniature popcorn-makers, in front of them. They snorted in unison.

"You really know how to take care business," he said, impressed.

Elijah felt slightly self-conscious horning cocaine in a room full of people, and she sensed it.

"Heyyyy, it's cool to do anything you want to do, up in here, this is Momma Mathews' turf."

They did the coke and sat back, side by side, checking out the party scene, sharing telepathic feelings.

201

A tall, well-built sister, obviously a dancer, began to move to the music, to give her rhythmic version of what she thought of things.

"Does she do that often?" Elijah asked, admiring her fluidity.

"Only when she doesn't feel like talkin'," Toni answered, clapping her hands together lightly, in tune with Olatunji. He leaned back on the bar, stylin', and checked the scene out completely.

A room full of people, people, wall to wall. A quintuplet of black fags doing a hora, passing the pipe around to members of their circle, obviously an In In group. A lush black lady, really lush, in the way that black women can be, posing against a vanilla-shaded wall, her darkness contrasting starkly with the wall, as half a dozen camera persons snapped and flashed their cameras on her young-Earth-Mother-figure. A David Bowie, white artist-freak-type dude, tailored by Savile Row, rapping with a black p.r. man . . . a deal? And a collection, beyond that, of poisoned pen holders, musicians, New World Africanists, psuedo counts 'n contessas, blackjack dealers, telephone starlets, slumming dishwashers, haiku salesmen and professional pickpockets.

Elijah was startled out of his dope reverie to discover that the man at his right side was embracing his woman, his . . . woman?!

Toni turned to Elijah with a coy expression on her face. "Elijah, this is Marcel Suchan, Marcel, this is . . . this is my good friend, Elijah Brookes, the First."

Elijah felt something weird happening when Marcel shook his hand, but couldn't really place where the feeling was coming from. "Enchante, M'sieur, and 'ow are you dewing?" the Frenchman asked, bowing slightly.

"Mellow here," Elijah responded, on guard.

Toni patted Marcel on the cheek and said playfully, "Give it all back . . . mind your manners, Marcel."

Elijah stared at the hand holding out his watch and wallet to him. A pickpocket! a super pickpocket!

"Pardon, Toni . . . Elijah . . . I was only . . . 'ow you say, practesein'? he seemed to be such a gud subject."

Elijah put his watch back on, smiling at Marcel. What the fuck else could you do but smile at a professional?

Marcel bowed grandly and eased back off into the crowd.

Elijah and Toni stared meaningfully at each other for a few seconds. So this is what your friends are like, huh?

She allowed him ten full minutes of taking it all in, waving or nodding to a friend from time to time, the number of people preventing any real hostessing from being done . . . a freeform set.

"Let's go somewhere a li'l quieter?" she suggested. Elijah nodded, not feeling the need for words.

She threaded her arm through his and made their way through the people stacked up in the room.

The couple on the bed turned toward the slit of light widening on them with impatience.

"Sorry 'bout that," Toni mumbled, closed the door with the air of a naughty little girl, and led Elijah down a long hall to another room. She pulled a trio of small keys out of her bolero jacket pocket. "If there's somebody in here, they're in trouble."

She unlocked the door to her combination library-office

and flicked on an old-fashioned desk lamp.

Elijah strolled in, his hands clasped behind his back, his thoughts triphammering. Who was the real Toni Mathews? What did she do? What was she into? Where was she coming from? What? How did she put all this together?

She sat on a long Danish modern sofa and watched him strolling around the room, his eyes darting from one book title to another.

"I don't have anything to taste on in here, if you want . . . ?"

"I'm cool. You got a lot o' books."

"A lot of them belonged to my husband."

"Your husband?" Now we gettin' somewhere.

"I was married, once upon a time."

Elijah sat comfortably close to light her cigarette and his, a question mark in both eyes.

Toni eyed him coolly, party sounds drifting in on them, not giving an inch more than she felt like giving.

Elijah, realizing that she was not going to be pumped about her past, slid off in another direction.

"You know, there's somethin' I been dyin' to ask you ever since we first met."

"What's that?"

"What were you doin' at that square ass party?"

"Someone asked me to go with him, so I went."

"I didn't see you with anyone."

"He'd gone to get me a drink."

"Oh wowwww! that must've been a cold shot for him when he got back and found you gone."

"Your friend must've been a li'l put out too, when she

204

looked around and couldn't find you."

They stared at each other for a minute, their senses of what was absurd and ridiculous polished by the cocaine, and then smiled, slyly . . . birds of a feather.

Elijah moved closer, casually draped his arm around her shoulder and stroked the side of her face.

"You knew I wanted to be your man the minute you laid eyes on me, didn't you?"

"Is that a question or a declaration?"

"Both."

She kissed his fingers . . . was the manicure working? . . . and undraped his arm.

"Are you sure you're ready for me? I'm built on a different scale than your girlfriend. What was her name?"

His frontal lobes throbbing from the effect of the drug, his sense of macho being taken on a trip, made Elijah flare up. "Hey! fuck her! we didn't come in here to talk about her, we came in here to talk about us."

"I travel in pretty fast company," Toni said quietly, ignoring his static.

"Yeah, yeah, I can see that. Is it all illegal?"

"Nope, none of it is," she replied in the same quiet voice. "I'm strictly on the up 'n up. What I'm concerned about is the dude in my life who's just tryin' to keep up, my man has to be out front."

Elijah felt a nervous spasm work through his right shoulder, the desire to smash his fist into her jaw flowing up and away. Who did this bitch think she was? Cleopatra or somebody?

Toni studied his reactions carefully.

"Look!" he finally burst out. "You say that to say what!? awright! awright! take me off into you li'l ol' thang if you want to. I was just askin' a real question, tryin' to get a real answer."

The continued calm in her voice made him seeth with anger. "Brothers be playin' games sometimes, Elijah. Some of 'em get off so far into games that they forget how to stop playin'. You know what I mean?"

The sincerity in his voice even surprised him, it had sunk to the same quiet level as Toni's. "Toni, I dig you. I know, comin' from a lot of people that wouldn't be meanin' too much . . . but, from me, it means a whole lot. Yeah, you right . . . a lotta brothers do be playin' games, but this one ain't . . . not this time anyway."

She nodded slowly, as though agreeing with him, and skirted back to answer an earlier question. "You were askin' me if what I did was illegal? like I said, no . . . I'm what you might call a hip square in business for herself."

Elijah, feeling like a player in some kind of abstract chess game, frowned. "A what?"

"A hip square, a businesswoman, in other words."

"Run it down to me."

"Nothing to run down. I have some connections that I use to help other people get ahead with, and myself in the bargain."

Elijah's frown lines deepened.

"I do p.r. work for several rock groups, a couple well-known stand-up comedians and, occasionally, as a favor, a guy named Billy Eckstein," she added with a sly smile.

Elijah slumped back on the sofa, his mouth forming a

large, round O.

"That all you got to say?"

"What else can I say, it's obvious that you on your job."

"Thought you might like to know how much I gross every month?"

Elijah stood up slowly, the coke making him feel taller, and started for the door. What sense did it make to be going through all these kinds of changes? He felt insulted because his honesty was being pissed on.

"Elijah?" She stood up and held her arms out to him.

He turned and hesitated. Was she playing a game? "Elijah, I'm sorry," she said, drifting to him. "I'm sorry, baby . . . you just get so used to protecting yourself sometimes that it's hard to stop. It's like I was sayin' about brothers playin' games? sisters get so caught up at protectin' ourselves from the games sometimes, that we don't know when to stop."

They stood, swaying in each other's arms, locked up.

"No, baby . . . this is no game, I'm fo' real," Elijah mumbled into her ear and squeezed a little more gently.

Yeahhh, Momma . . . I'm gon' get my shit together for you . . . yessuhhhh . . .

CHAPTER 12

Elijah peeked around the shoulder of the woman in front of him, number four in line.

Damn! what's taking so long?

He gazed around the airport lobby, trying to look non-chalant, just a dude with a stolen airlines credit card, doin' a li'l number.

"Heyyy, 'Lijah baby, gimme fifty for this?" Li'l Bruh, the dope fiend's dope fiend, had asked, knowing that he would never put the card to any use, and had accepted twenty grudgingly, one foot shuffling off to the pusher before the money was in his hand good. Another five was enough to buy the wallet and the identification papers that it contained. What did Li'l Bruh care? He was satisfied with the eighty-five he had pulled out of it . . . a double score for a score.

It had only taken Elijah a few seconds of close questioning to find out that the card had only been ripped off hours before; Li'l Bruh was never more than two hours before, or two hours after any theft, which made him an ideal to deal with.

Elijah's first impulse was to put the card on the open market himself, but, feeling romantic, he decided to work it a bit before passing it on.

He pushed his shades up on his nose and fingered the tips of his shirt collar. Wonder what kind of reaction I'll get when I plunk two tickets to Jamaica down in front of her?

"Be rally great to get out of the country for a while, won't it, fella?"

"Huh?" Elijah responded, torn out of his dream-thought.

"I said . . ." the voice started to repeat.

"Oh yeah, really!" Elijah cut him off, too nervous for small talk, and moved two steps closer, number three now.

He half turned for a peripheral look at the dude who'd spoken to him.

Large, square, broken veins in his nose, what was it they called dudes like him? Ruddy? yeah, he was ruddy, half-ass rich. "Be rally great to get out of the country for a while, won't it?"

You motherfucker you! If it hadn't been for motherless bastards like you I never would've been in this fucked-up place in the first place.

The man behind checked out the sideward glance being laid on him and acknowledged it with a benevolent smile.

Elijah frowned and snapped his eyes forward. Number two now. The svelte, understated pantsuit in the Dache hat leaned both elbows up on the counter and slid from one patronizing attitude to another with the reservations person, a Scandinavian type with cold blue eyes and a warm, fixed smile.

Elijah, taking advantage of the hostility being generated in front of him, smiled superpleasantly around the Dache hat's shoulder.

The Scandinavian smiled back, her eyes glittering like ice cubes, digging on his appreciation of the shit she had to deal with.

Finally it was his turn. He stepped forward and removed his shades, the model nigger dealing with a blonde white-white woman, 1974 variety, on both sides.

"Hi, how are *you* today?" The brighter-than-white smile glistening out of her mahogany tan, into his naturally brown one.

"Fine, fine," nodding his head after the Dache hat. "Givin' ya a rough time, huh?"

Blue eyes rolled momentarily skyward in theatrical exasperation. "Aw, well, you know how it is, some people want you to give them service and . . . well . . ."

Fake joviality. "Hahhahhah, I can dig it. Uhh, the name is Louis Michaels, I have reservations for two on your ten-fifteen flight to Kingston, in Jamaica."

The blue eyes melted for a second, memories of what it felt like to be a blonde-blonde, in Kingston, in sixty-two.

"The party flight, huh?"

"The what?"

"The party flight. That's what everybody calls it, you know? what with the rum 'n all."

"Oh, uh, right on! hahhahhah."

He tried to twist his eyes upside down as she began to write. "Michaels? that's Mi-ch-ae-ls?"

"Right! first name Louis, Lo-u-is."

They both tripped quickly through the prosaic business of her writing out the two ticket forms, each of them playing his role as though they had been rehearsing for days.

Elijah looked down at the card between his thumb and forefinger and, for a split second, panicked, thinking . . . nawww, this'll never work, somebody's goin' to pop out of the woodwork and do me in. But his nerves steadied themselves on an old hustler's proverb, you can't cheat an honest man. And Lawd knows there's no more a corrupt system in the world than the one I'm rippin' at right now.

The reservations clerk treated his card unremarkably and explained, with the patience born of many such explanations, exactly what time he should be at gate ten to board the ten-fifteen.

Elijah nodded calmly to it all. Wowwww! I'm gettin' away with it! I'm gettin' away with it!

He clapped a lascivious nod and wink on the Scandinavian and strutted away, his mental energies concentrated now on selling the credit card itself, as quickly as possible.

His mind buzzing, he stomped through the automatic opening doors. Lemme see . . . reschedule the flight for Saturday, that'll give me time to see if Toni's head is at gettin' it righteously on or not.

"Elijah, I'll go and do what my man wants to do. If he says, let's go sit on the curb 'n spit watermelon seeds in the gutter, that's what we'll be doin'. I'm with my man."

He hummed a few stray bars of "Matilda" on his way to the airport parking lot.

"Remove your parking ticket and lock your car, please, thank you." The continuous announcement cut into his humming, made him smile. Wonder how they say that in Jamaican?

Having carefully placed the information on the wire in the early afternoon that he had a "clean" airline credit card, he had made contact with a buyer in the late afternoon, and now, at ten p.m., sat in the Afro Lounge, sipping and waiting for his "client."

The well-shaved brother with no dip to his knees, no sly movement of his hands or shoulders, and nothing spectacular on his back, caused several of the regulars to double-check him. Elijah gave the bartender an eye sign that the dude was cool, that she could tell him which one was Elijah. She directed him to Elijah's table with a casual nod of her chin.

"Uhh, pardon me, may I join you?" the man asked.

Elijah felt like laughing in his face, the dude had obviously gotten into how-to-do-illegal-things from watching the late late show. Uhhh, pardon me, may I join you? Wowww, where is the brother comin' from?

Seeing that it would shoot matters along, Elijah decided to get down for the square's sake.

"Yeahhh, go 'head, sit down," he mumbled, looking off.

The man sat across from Elijah, trying to give a casual impression of himself, but failed miserably, he was obviously up tight.

"Uh, you are Mr. Brookes, are you not?"

"Uhhh, I think so," Elijah put him on, crinkling his forehead, "but sometimes I doubt it. You must be Monroe."

Paul Monroe, a martini sipper, Beefeater only, university grad, doubles player and a pretender to upper crustic origins, pushed his horn rims up on his nose and looked around quickly. *Well, it wouldn't be too likely that anyone I know would be in a place like this.*

"Ahhemm, yes, my name is Monroe. You have the . . . uh . . . 'ticket' for sale?"

"You got a grand, Monroe?"

Monroe felt around inside his collar, so good a caricature of Peter Lorre in desperate straits that Elijah almost laughed aloud. "Yes, yes, I have it."

Elijah stood up. "I'm goin' the shithouse, follow me in a couple minutes."

For the regulars, who knew that something was going down, but not exactly what, Elijah's play was hip drama.

He fired up a joint in the men's room and leaned in Chink's spot beside the barred window.

Two tickets to Jamaica and a grand, plus a dynamite lady. How much better could it be?

He stared up at the sky through the bars for a few seconds. *Gotta get Browney off my back . . . maybe I'll stay in Jamaica.*

Monroe walked in stiffly, squinching up his nose at the rank smells.

"Awright, what can I do for you, bruh?" Elijah teased him, coming close to blowin' a stream of smoke in his face.

Monroe's paranoia almost caused him to step back, away

213

from Elijah, the Afro Lounge, the hostile black faces in the bar, the neighborhood he was in, the ghetto, everything. "The card you have for sale?" he asked quickly, greed overcoming his paranoia.

"Here it is." Elijah held it out to him.

Monroe whipped a long, white envelope out of his breast pocket. "Here's the money."

"Lemme see it, shit! that ain't nothin' but a fuckin' envelope!"

Monroe grimaced, fumbled the flap open and nervously counted through nine hundred-dollar bills and two fifties.

Elijah sucked in a deep hit and jetted the smoke into Monroe's face as he accepted the money. "Bon voyage," he said, in a low, sinister voice.

Monroe's eyes buckled once, twice, and he was gone, practically racing back to a car that had been gleaned of its tape setup, hubcaps and battery.

Elijah, a dead, high, calm in him, paused to squeeze a blackhead from his left cheek, richer by a grand of untaxable money.

Monroe. What makes a dude like Monroe tick? scared as any white man in the deep ghetto after dark. And . . . what the hell can he actually do with that card? What's it matter? I got the money 'n he got the card.

Yeahhh, I got the money 'n he's got the card. I bet that booshie ass nigger can get that card doctored up a li'l and use it for a whole bunch of things.

He made his re-appearance, to the sound of silent, visual applause, keeping a cool front, but seriously wondering now, if he had just been ripped off.

214

Oh well, you win some and lose a few.

He leaned his chin into his palm, a cigarette in the other hand, fascinated by the sight of the city gently revolving before his eyes.

Having lunch with Toni. Having lunch with Toni in the Round Wheel, the revolving restaurant that tried to give a clear view of every part of town except the black part. Downtown, slightly north. Having lunch? Boy, you really gettin' up in the world . . . used to be a time when every meal was called just that, a meal, except breakfast, if there was any.

He stared at her as though she were a stranger as she coolly wove through the maze of white-covered tables, a beautifully dark vision in saffron and creme de menthe.

She really is a beautiful black woman and she's mine . . . all mine.

"What're you sittin' here daydreamin' about?" she asked, gracefully reoccupying her place across from him.

"I wasn't daydreamin', I was beginnin' to wonder if you were constipated or somethin'."

She playfully spanked his hand. "Elijah! you're terrible! Worse than a bad li'l boy, at times. I was powdering my nose, that's what girls do when they go to the powder room."

"They also take a shit too, every now 'n then."

Elijah spoke loud enough for an elderly white couple across from them to hear, the kind who say, "My word!" and "Oh dear!" when they get pissed off. They slanted identical frowns across at them, pissed off by Elijah's language.

Toni and Elijah, a li'l bit of the naughty boy in each of them, leaned their heads close together and giggled.

"May I take your order now, sir?"

"Uhh, yes, we'd like two more margueritas."

The waiter tipped Elijah a slight European bow, from habit, and strode away frowning. Six margueritas already! Don't they know about the famous Round Wheel T-bone? The baked Idaho potato with tub butter and sour cream? with chives yet?

The giggles gave way to smiles, the smiles were replaced by solemn, soulful expressions. They sat, watching the world turn, not saying anything for a minute, oblivious to the unreal world around them, aware that they were into another realm of feeling.

The waiter placed the drinks in front of them. "Would you care to . . . ?"

"Later," Elijah said out of the corner of his mouth, his eyes dancing with Toni's lips, her cheekbones, her nose, her eyes, the narrow trail between her full breasts.

"Yes, of course, sir . . . whenever you are ready."

"They must think we're lushes," Toni whispered, watching the waiter march away.

"I don't care what they think. Listen, I have an idea."

"What is it?" she asked, sipping.

"I've been up half the night and I'm pretty tired . . . yawnnnn . . . why don't we go to my place?"

"You ain't sleepy, nigger," she practically purred across the table. "You just want to play with my body."

"Call me Sweet Nigger when you talk like that," he shot back at her, an In joke established between them.

I just wanna play with your body, huh? he spoke to her with his eyes, high from the tequila but drunk on her. Remember the first time? his eyes asked . . . at the party? in the library? on the floor. And the other time, and after that, the next time, up 'til there was no way to keep track.

Yeahhh, baby . . . I wanna play with your body. I want to lick it all over, go deeper into you than I've ever wanted to go into any woman. I want to play a new tune on you.

I just want to play with your body? shit! that don't even get close to what I want to do with you.

He licked the salt from the rim of his glass, took a sip, and cupped his hands under his glass, as though he were cradling both cheeks of her buttocks in his palms.

The gesture made her feel self-conscious enough to want to change the unspoken subject. "Elijah, don't you ever get tired of playin' games?"

The corners of his mouth sagged. Don't tell me that you gon' take me through your li'l ol' thang again. I thought we had finished with all that.

"What do you mean?" he asked cautiously, a bit of the spell broken.

"You know what I mean, baby," she cushioned it. "Playin' games on people."

"When I get tired of eatin'—" He patted his flat stomach. "Then I'll be tired of playin' games."

Damn! damn it! why did I ever break down and tell her what I do, what I really do? Home was right, a man will do anything when he gets his nose open.

"You ever think about gettin' into anything . . . anything legitimate?"

He drained his glass and caught the waiter's eye to signal for a fresh round. Is she talkin' to me about gettin' a job?

"What're you talkin' about, Toni? gettin' a job?" he voiced his thought, on the edge of hostility.

"No, not just a job . . . something that would allow you to use your talents, and not run the risk of being popped."

He felt his hostile reactions being cancelled out, one by one. She was right, about being popped. That's the way it always seemed to happen.

Just when the whole thing seemed to be falling into place, Pop! He counted back through a dozen games that had been worked successfully until . . . Pop!

If they couldn't get the goods on him, they could shelter him on a jive time vagrancy beef . . . with his rep and sheet, what the hell did it matter?

The waiter suavely cleared the old glasses away and replaced them with fresh ones, reconciled to the fact that he had drinkers and not eaters on his station.

"Yeah, I've thought about a legitimate thang, from time to time." He paused for a sip and discovered he was drunk. Hip, stoned drunk, not square, goofy drunk . . . rappin' drunk.

"Yeah, a legitimate thang, something I could put my talents to, as you put it. But, dig, you know what I came up with, in terms of really gettin' off into it? Z-ro!

"Number one." he paused for another sip, trying to figure out where he was going as he talked.

Toni had an absorbed expression on her face, like, speak! say something about what's on your mind!

"Okay! I can read a mark, I can con a lady, I can milk a

feelin' to the bone. Sometimes, when I feel super unusual on my job, I can damn near become invisible. But none of this kind of shit is employable. Can you dig where I'm comin' from, Toni?"

She nodded slowly, her mind on the love she felt for him, Sweet Nigger. "But, Elijah," she started off, knowing that he would never give her a chance to carry on, now that he was tuned up.

"Naw! naw! lissen t' me, baby . . . you can sniff up your nose at games, but it's one of the few kinds of thangs that people seem to really want to be into. Like, okay, dig it! a sucker will go off from his ol' lady for a few hours and rent out a pussy. The ho whose sellin' the trick the trim is really not runnin' a game on the trick, the trick is trickin' himself into believin' that he's buyin' some love. Awright, that one kind o' scene. In my situation—" He felt like screaming—"in my situation, I know that I'm offerin' a simple, human, public service to a large number of people who need it. I ain't bein' funny either, I mean it! I know, in my soul, that there is as much a need for streetologists, who take advantage of mentally displaced persons, as there is for psychologists, who don't offer half as much hope, most of the time."

Toni leaned back in her seat, loving him, not really caring, behind her fourth marguerita, what he was talking about.

"Shit! you talk about legitimate thangs!? I've probably been on top of one of the most legitimate things happenin' in this country for years, which is . . . ill-legitimacy! That means, if you can dig where I'm comin' from? that I'm offerin' an out. If the thing that you're doin', or that's doin' you too much, then what I'm doin' is offerin' a middle ground . . . somethin' that may offer you a cloud bed in the sky, or a hard crust of nails, whichever it is that pleases you. And, heyyy, let's face it, baby . . . lots o' people need these kinds of alternatives, escapes.

"Everything ain't just black 'n white, a lot of people are very much in tune with gray, which is what a lot of people would call cheatin', but which really ain't, because, sometimes, cheatin' is just another means of keepin' the faith."

Toni signalled to the waiter, knowing, from the look on his stolid, Teutonic face, that he would be disappointed that they were not going from drink to food, but then, he didn't know niggers too well. How could he? the subject being as new as it was.

Elijah plunged into his wallet, anxious to show the world around him that he meant to care for, and not be cared for.

"Elijah?" Toni slurred at him, "why don't we go over to your place? I'm tired."

Elijah doubled the waiter's tip and carefully made his way out of the restaurant behind Toni, new thoughts on his mind, inspired by his own rap.

CHAPTER 13

"Jamaica?!"

"Yeah, baby, Jamaica!"

The look in her face had bordered on the incredible. Jamaica!? He had been forced to explain how the whole thing had come about, and, as a topping, that he had done it all for her.

Her loving, in response to the gift of a Jamaican holiday, had been exceptionally special. Profound. Or maybe it had been the margueritas.

"Elijah, are you sure those people ain't gonna pull us off the plane and stick us in jail?"

"Not a chance, sweetthang. Dig it, the dude that the card was ripped off from, had it ripped off without him knowin' it, and when he finds out he won't be able to report it."

"Why?"

"Well, for two big reasons, number one, he's dealin', 'n

221

number two, he had it ripped off while he was layin' up. Believe me, baby, everything is cool. The word is out now, he wants his wallet 'n stuff back and he's offerin' five hundred for it. He won't know about the trip until he's billed at the end of the month."

"I don't know, Elijah . . . I just don't know, I'll have to give it a li'l thought."

"What's there to think about? We'll go down 'n lay up in the sun for a bit . . . and start talkin' about some kinda future for us."

"Let me think on it for a day or so, okay?"

He shot past the Afro Lounge, in deep thought, his spirits high, coin in pocket, feeling groovy.

He spun around the corner and past the lounge again, feeling the urge to share his good vibes with someone he knew, anybody.

Parking on the side street, hearing much less noise than usual, made him feel uneasy, vaguely apprehensive. He got out of his car, probing the possibilities of what life would be like with Toni.

She's really a sho' 'nuff dynamite sister.

"Elijah?" the voice called softly from a dark doorway.

"Nawww, this is Phil, man," Elijah answered, immediately slipping into a role. Sounds like . . .

"Don't gimme that shit! I know 'Lijah Brookes when I see 'im!"

Bennie. Bennie the Bandit. Yeahhh, that's who it would be. "You got the wrong dude, brotherman."

Bennie tilted his hat back off his face as he stepped into the soft gleam of a streetlight.

"What makes you think that?"

Elijah stared at Bennie's face, a cold network of lines and scars. "Well, I'll be damned! my ol' buddy!" Elijah conned, trying to edge closer, to get an angle to work from.

Bennie pulled a large, ugly German luger from his belt. "Awww, no you don't! don't be givin' me that ol' buddy bullshit!"

Elijah, conning harder, folded his arms across his chest and laid a super-stern glare on Bennie.

"Heyyyy, what's happenin', brother? . . . I thought we settled our beef a while back."

"They sent me for the rest of the dough," Bennie spoke in a low, determined voice, ignoring Elijah's question.

"They who, brotherman?"

"You know who! you got it!?"

Elijah edged a step at a time across the narrow expanse of sidewalk between himself and Bennie.

"Listen to me, sucker . . . what're you gon' be, the white boy's errand boy? how much did they give you to come for your brother, 'brother'?"

"It didn't take too much, not to come for your rotten ass!"

Bennie's reflexes jerked off two rounds into Elijah's chest as the right hand whistled past his jaw.

Both men stumbled back from each other as though they were figures in a bad dream.

"You chickenshit . . ." Elijah started a sentence he couldn't finish and slumped to the sidewalk.

"Hey! what's goin' on down there?!" a voice called out from one of the buildings around them.

Bennie stepped closer to rob Elijah but found his cold, wolfish grin too much to deal with. He kicked at Elijah's head and missed . . . the head, in death, seeming to dodge.

"What's happenin' down there!?" another voice called out . . . the neighborhood waking up to discover another killing.

Bennie made another attempt to kick Elijah's face in, missed, and started moving away at a swift trot, afraid to attempt to deal with Elijah Brookes, the First, any more.

A pall hung over the atmosphere in the Afro Lounge, the grapevine bringing, in its own supersonic fashion, word of Elijah's death. The Toe, Leelah, Nick the Geech, Sid the Shark and several of the regular regulars, the bona fide fast people, looked off into faraway places, remembering.

"I hear he had close to nine thousand dollars on him when . . ." Whispers, the legend being formed . . .

Precious Percy, currently bitchless, but inevitably optimistic, working on an ex-cotton picker from Arkansas, strolled in, took a close reading of the scene and ordered a round for the house.

"I don't know what you niggers sittin' 'round here lookin' down in the mouth about, 'Lijah ain't dead, that motherfucker probably had somebody knocked off that looked like him . . . so, so he could go off somewhere 'n get another kind o' game together."

Leelah's head sank with grief as she watched Precious Percy shuffle out of the Afro Lounge, tears glistening in his eyes.

Time out!